The Astronomer

Wood crashed, and glass shattered. Startled, Norman peered about in an effort to find the source of the new disturbance. The bootlegger did the same, then hastily backpedaled out of sight. As he disappeared, he raised his pistol and fired upward.

Ahead of Norman and to his right, stacks of crates swayed. Dark shapes leaped to the stacks on the left in what seemed to be a pursuit of the gunman. The forms were sufficiently high above Norman's flashlight beam and departed so quickly that his eyes registered nothing more than a surge of movement. But their mass and the vigor of their springing dislodged the upper boxes, and the crates smashed to the floor.

More shots rang out. Additional crates fell. Silence followed. Norman crept up to the intersection and peered around the corner.

There was nothing to see but a splash of light where the bootlegger had tried to retreat down a different aisle. The glow wasn't dimming however, which meant both the lantern, and the man who carried it, had stopped moving. Norman imagined the man lying torn and dead with *something* crouching over him.

Surely poor Schmidt had been the first to die. Norman would be crazy to linger in this place a moment longer.

Cover illustration by Shane Pierce.

Color insert artwork by Kristina Carroll, Reiko Murakami, and Chris Ostrowski.

ISBN: 978-1-63344-316-7

Printed in China.

Fantasy Flight Games
1995 West County Road B2
Roseville, MN 55113
USA

Find out more about Fantasy Flight Games
and our many exciting worlds at

www.FantasyFlightGames.com

An

ARKHAM
HORROR™

Novella

Ire of the Void
by Richard Lee Byers

Fantasy Flight Games

Welcome to Arkham

IT IS THE HEIGHT OF THE ROARING TWENTIES. Flappers and young fellas dance the Charleston at raucous jazz clubs gleaming bright with electric lights. Beneath this gilded glamour, bloody turf wars rage, funded by gangsters and crooked cops who frequent rival speakeasies and gambling dens.

Amid these changing times, old New England towns hold their secrets close. Off the Aylesbury Pike, in reclusive Dunwich, rolling hills hide decrepit farms and witch-haunted hollows. Past Cape Ann, the remote fishing village of Innsmouth rots from within. At the mouth of the Miskatonic River, mist-shrouded Kingsport lies dreaming. All the while, historic Arkham broods on the upper banks of the Miskatonic, its famed university delving into the world's darkest, most ancient mysteries.

Arkham's citizens insist everything is normal in their sleepy town, but horrific and bizarre events occur with increasing frequency. Strange lights flicker and people disappear in the forest beyond Hangman's Brook. Misshapen silhouettes prowl graveyards and shorelines, leaving savaged corpses in their wake. Nightmarish artifacts and disturbing tomes have surfaced, chronicling gods and incantations the world has tried to forget. Cavalier scientists have glimpsed far-flung worlds beyond our own that shatter the known laws of reality. Are these events somehow connected? If so, what calamity do they portend?

Those who dare investigate these incidents witness the inexplicable. Having seen such phenomena, they can never regain their old view of the world. Now that they know the hideous truth, they cannot run or hide from it. Just beneath the reassuring veneer of reality—a veneer that was never meant to be worn away—are forces that can drive the average person to despair. Yet, a rare few try to avert the end of the world, knowing it may well cost them their lives or sanity.

These investigators must rely on their wits and skills to learn as much as they can before it's too late. Some may find courage in the grace of a rosary, while others may burn away their fears with a swig of bootleg whiskey. They must try their hand at unpredictable spells that could doom them, or take up rifles and revolvers to combat foul creatures plaguing the night. Will it be enough?

Part One
The Barn

Norman Withers was accustomed to empty seats. He was not a popular instructor, he did not take attendance, and his lectures were redundant with the textbook. Still, today, the classroom was emptier than usual, and for no reason he could think of.

"Mr. Davison," he said, addressing a perpetually sweaty, twitchy student who never missed a single one of Norman's classes or, in all likelihood, any other professor's.

Davison gave a start as if he had been caught doing something reprehensible instead of paying scrupulous attention and writing copious notes. "Yes, sir?" he squeaked.

"Where is everyone? Is something else going on today?"

"Well, sir, Claus Schmidt is giving a guest lecture. I think some people went to hear him." The boy cringed as though he feared Norman would be offended and take out the resentment on him.

In truth, even had Norman been so inclined, he was too busy feeling shocked that he'd heard nothing of this to bother with such a vindictive response. Perhaps, as the secretaries were forever scolding him, he should check the cubbyhole that was his faculty mailbox on days other than payday.

"*The* Claus Schmidt?" he asked. "The one who collaborates with Albert Einstein?"

If so, this was the physicist widely acclaimed as Einstein's brilliant young protégé. While still working toward his doctorate, Schmidt had participated in Eddington's expedition that provided observational verification of general relativity, and had since aided Einstein himself in calculating the cosmological constant and establishing relativistic cosmology. It was extraordinary that such a luminary—a European luminary, at that—had suddenly materialized in Arkham, Massachusetts.

"Yes, sir," Davison said.

"Where is he speaking? The big auditorium in the Science building?"

"Yes, sir."

"Class dismissed."

Norman hurried from the classroom ahead of any of his students, rushed past the foundation for the new observatory, and broke into a run at the Miskatonic University quad, breezing by its silver maples and sycamores. Strolling or lounging on benches, young scholars smirked or chuckled as he dashed past.

Their amusement prompted him to duck into one of the Science building's men's rooms and try to make himself presentable. The mirror showed a scarecrow of a man. His scraggly white beard needed trimming, and his hair stuck up every which way. His tie was loose and askew, and his tweed suit had gone weeks without a pressing.

It was too late to remedy all of that, but he would do the best he could. He reached into his pocket, found he had no comb, and smoothed down his hair with his hand. Then he fixed his tie, straightened his lapels, and proceeded to the auditorium. As he reached for the door, laughter pealed on the other side. Apparently the young physicist seasoned his lectures with humor.

Norman found a seat in the back of the hall. Claus Schmidt was a stout, cheerful-looking young man dressed in what was, for a scientist, a surprisingly stylish Lindbergh jacket. His English was excellent, only lightly accented, and he clearly relished American slang, slipping terms like "razz" and "bushwa" into his discourse.

Taken altogether, the jokes, the slang, and his friendly, animated manner made his subject matter all the more accessible. He was speaking on Theodor Kaluza's attempt to extend general relativity into five dimensions—an abstruse topic to say the least, but he was clearly holding his audience's attention.

The lecturer concluded to enthusiastic applause. A significant portion of the audience rose from their seats and headed for the front of the auditorium to congratulate him. Although he tried not to be *completely* rude about it, Norman elicited glowers and complaints as he squeezed and jostled forward. He did not want the physicist to disappear through one of the side exits before he reached him.

As he neared the podium, the German said, "I didn't come here expecting to lecture. I hope I didn't ball it up."

Professor Grant smiled, his bald crown gleaming, spectacles slipped halfway down a prominent nose. "It was wonderful. Now, can we offer you some lunch? The roast beef in the Faculty Club is excellent."

"*Danke,*" said Schmidt, "thank you, but I really should be about my business. If you found me a car and driver—"

"I'll drive you!" Norman called.

Grant and several other faculty members turned to eye him askance. The bald academic cleared his throat. "That is kind of you, Professor Norman. But someone has already made arrangements."

Norman turned to the youthful Schmidt in his modish clothes. "I know Arkham. Wherever you're going, I'll get you there and take you in style. I've got a Stutz Bearcat." The sports car was left over from better times when he—and his wife—took pleasure in such extravagances.

Schmidt's blue eyes opened wide. "Is it a breezer?"

"It is indeed."

The physicist turned back to Grant. "Thank you for all you've done. But since Professor…Norman, is it?…is here now, offering, I might as well take him up on it."

Grant grimaced. "Well, should there be a problem…that is to say, should you require another driver for any reason, just let me know."

• • •

Richard Lee Byers

═ 2 ═

Norman had not lowered the Bearcat's canvas top in years. But it was a mild, sunny September day, and his companion was excited that the two-seater with its doghouse hood was a convertible, so he fumbled his way through the half-forgotten procedure.

Schmidt stowed a black leather valise in the trunk and then handed Norman a list of addresses. "In any order," he said. "Whatever's convenient."

There was nothing about the list to indicate why the German was interested in these particular locations. Norman supposed Schmidt would enlighten him in due course. "We might as well start in Southside and work our way north," he said.

Once the trip was underway, Schmidt availed himself of the unobstructed view to take in the city's Georgian houses with their dentilwork cornices, side-gabled or gambrel roofs, and double chimneys. "Charming," he said.

"I suppose," Norman said, "at the moment." When he thought of Arkham, he thought of gray skies, gray walls, and decay.

Schmidt chuckled at Norman's dour tone. "So level with me, old boy. Why didn't Grant and those others want you to drive me? What's their beef?"

Norman winced. "I am not sure what you mean."

"Tell it to Sweeney! You're on the outs. So am I, back home. That's why I came with you. Well, that and the car. I'll tell you about it, but you go first."

Norman needed to confide in the younger man, or Schmidt could not possibly help him. Even so, he felt reluctant. It was pleasant being in the company of a colleague who did not see him as eccentric, if not unhinged. It would pain him to lose the physicist's good opinion if that was how things worked out.

Peering squarely through the sports car's monocle windshield—so as not to see how Schmidt reacted to his story—he took a long breath and began. "I am an astronomer. Some of my work involves discovering and cataloging new stars. On March 11th, 1916, I found six faint stars in the vicinity of Canis Major. Then they vanished all at once, literally within seconds of one another, and have never reappeared."

"Given interstellar distances," Schmidt said, "I don't know of a phenomenon to account for that."

"Nor do I," Norman said. "Nor did anyone. Without exception, other astronomers deemed it more plausible that I never really observed the stars in the first place. Eyestrain, they said. Smudges. Meteors. But I know what I saw!"

"And you've never been able to let it go," said Schmidt.

"It's that obvious, is it? Yes, I never stopped looking for the answer, and it's blighted my scientific reputation. I don't suppose I'd have retained my position at Miskatonic if not for tenure and the fact that I still put in time doing conventional research and publish the occasional journal article."

He could have added that as he had grown increasingly obsessed with the mystery, it had blighted his marriage as well. Eventually, Bernadine divorced him and moved to Los Angeles to be near their daughter, but why pick at that wound? It would only make him look even more pathetic than he likely appeared already.

"If the vanishing stars are the focus of your work," said Schmidt, "and you were so eager to make contact with me, then you must believe I can help you somehow."

"Yes. You—you, Einstein, your circle—are discovering revolutionary new truths about the workings of the universe. I hoped that if I prevailed on you to consider my findings, you'd have some fresh insight to offer."

"I have to confess, nothing is springing to mind. But you're helping with my research. Afterward, it seems only fair that I take a serious look at yours. Then we'll see if I might actually be able to contribute."

Norman hesitated. "I hope you aren't just humoring me. If you think I'm babbling nonsense, you can say it."

"But I don't think it, or at least I don't *assume* it. Now that I've been told that my own current line of research is a load of horse-feathers, I'm less inclined to dismiss the ideas of others out of hand."

Norman pulled the brake lever at one of Arkham's four electric traffic signals, erected two years previously. "What is that line of research? I have to say, I am puzzled as to what problem of physics is better investigated driving around Miskatonic County than in your laboratory in Berlin."

"How familiar are you with general relativity?"

"Reasonably so. Your discipline is relevant to mine." The traffic signal turned green. Norman waited for a horse-drawn wagon to clear the intersection, then put the Bearcat in gear.

"Then you know the theory connects the curvature of space-time to the density of mass in the vicinity. To gravity."

"Yes. By so doing, it explains the anomalous perihelion advance of Mercury and the deflection of starlight Eddington observed during the solar eclipse of '19."

"Exactly. My own scientific heresy has been to connect the idea that space-time can be curved, twisted, warped not just to what we observe in the sky but also to phenomena here on Earth. People disappear mysteriously. Sometimes they even appear just as strangely, peculiar souls who don't seem to belong in the times or places in which they're discovered. If there are discontinuities— folds or holes—in the structure of reality, people could blunder into them and find themselves transported."

Norman frowned. "Surely these disappearances are either legends or events that, were we privy to all the facts, would prove to have a mundane explanation."

"There are more such incidents than you may suppose, in every land and era, and some have been extensively studied without any convincing explanation emerging."

"Well…fair enough, I suppose. But unless I misunderstand them entirely, Einstein's field equations don't allow for the extreme distortions you're proposing. Not on a body with the mass of the Earth, and not at one point on the surface but not another."

"But what," Schmidt asked, "if general relativity, though predictive at a certain level just as Newton's laws are, is similarly incomplete? What if something other than mass is also capable of bending space-time? I hope to prove it is, and then science can figure out the what and the how."

"And you can prove this by touring Arkham?"

Schmidt smiled. "I hope so, old boy, because of your history. You may not realize it, but since the town was founded it has had an amazing number of unexplained disappearances. My plan is to collect data in the places where they happened."

Norman mulled that over. "This was your 'scientific heresy.'"

"Einstein is sure it's applesauce. But he can't be right *all* the time, can he?"

Perhaps not, but in this instance the eminent physicist seemed far more likely to be right than his protégé. Norman sighed at the realization that Schmidt could not really help him after all. Once, conceivably, but not now that he had given himself over to nonsensical pseudoscience. Perhaps it was not too late to make an excuse, foist the German off on the driver Professor Grant had offered, and salvage the rest of the day.

Suddenly, it occurred to Norman that he was dismissing Schmidt exactly as his fellow astronomers dismissed him, and for pursuing a line of investigation arguably no unlikelier than his own.

Damn it, he wasn't going to be like them! Not because he believed Schmidt's notions were correct, but because the young man's attitude was. A scientist shouldn't bow down to an argument from authority, even if the authority was Albert Einstein. He should go where his instincts led him and collect evidence to confirm or deny a hypothesis.

Besides, it was pleasant driving the Bearcat around on a sunny day with the top down. He had forgotten. He was a bit sorry when he and Schmidt arrived at the first spot on their itinerary.

= 3 =

The old house stood with the steeple of South Church peeking over the hipped roof like a priest suspicious that someone was robbing the poor box. Even under a blue sky, the structure's appearance was in accord with Norman's impression of Arkham as a crumbling, decrepit habitation. Sickly yellow paint peeled from the clapboards, and the multi-pane windows were grimy. One was cracked.

As soon as Norman pulled up at the curb, Schmidt jumped out of the Bearcat. "Open the trunk!"

For a moment, a smile tugged at the corners of Norman's mouth. His companion was as impatient as a child at the entrance to a carnival. "I take it you have high hopes for this place."

"In 1774," Schmidt replied, "responding to the Suffolk Resolves, five of Arkham's community leaders entered a room in this house to discuss the organization of a militia and never came out. That's the space we're going to investigate."

Norman was half-embarrassed, half-amused that he did not know what the Suffolk Resolves were when a foreigner did. He picked up the valise, and metal clinked inside it. As he carried it toward the portico, he spotted the sign beside the panel door: *Apartments for Rent.*

"If someone has altered the floor plan—"

"We should still be able to identify the right spot," Schmidt replied. "We just need a little luck." He opened the door, stepped into a foyer, and headed down the hallway that ran past a staircase toward the rear of the building. "I think we want the last door on the right."

A tinny radio was playing "Riverboat Shuffle," as performed by Bix Beiderbecke and the Wolverines, on the other side of the door, which had a brass number 5 screwed onto it. Schmidt knocked, and after a moment a small woman with a face like a fist and mouse-brown hair in curlers responded.

"Good evening, madam," said Schmidt. "My colleague and I are scientists from the university. We're conducting research that requires us to take some readings in your home. I promise it won't take long, and we'll leave everything as we found it."

The woman scowled. "Mr. Page—my husband—says never let anyone in when he's not here." She started to close the door.

Schmidt whisked a folded dollar bill from his pocket. "Naturally, we wouldn't dream of asking without offering to compensate you for your trouble."

Mrs. Page hesitated. "I'd have to leave the door open."

"Of course," said Schmidt.

She grabbed the money. The physicist shot Norman a wink as the door swung open.

The cramped apartment seemed an unlikely place for a scientific breakthrough, but Schmidt's enthusiasm remained undiminished. He took the bag from Norman, flipped up the latches, and brought out a thermometer. He then moved about the apartment, repeatedly stopping and recording the temperature in various spots. Mrs. Page regarded him with perplexity writ large on her pinched, blotchy face.

Norman knew how she felt. "What does this have to do with space-time?" he asked at length.

Schmidt shrugged. "I had a hunch. Maybe it was wrong, or maybe the differential is so slight the thermometer can't detect it. Either way, what comes next is more important."

He returned to the valise and produced a carpenter's level and squares of cardboard. Inserting the latter under the legs of Mrs. Page's dining room table as needed, he rendered it rock-steady despite the uneven flooring beneath.

After that, he brought out a small triple beam balance scale, set it on the table, and put a lead one-gram weight on the platform. Unsurprisingly, it turned out to weigh one gram.

Despite himself, Norman felt his earlier disgruntlement creeping back. He had not known what to expect, but surely a revolutionary discovery in physics required more than pointless fiddling with the most basic of instruments.

Then again, Einstein had supposedly arrived at his extraordinary insights through thought alone. After all, a telescope was simply pieces of glass in a tube, and now that Norman had come this far, what did he have to lose by seeing the venture through? If it all turned out to be "bushwa," he could at least take comfort that, for once, he wasn't the one who looked the fool.

"What did that accomplish?"

"Nothing yet," Schmidt answered, "but now we move the table. We'll have to re-level it with each placement."

"I would assume so." Norman took hold of an end.

They shifted the table about, and for the first half-dozen placements, one gram was one gram. Then, when the platform was partway across the yellowed linoleum floor of the kitchen, the weight registered ever so slightly less. Schmidt crowed and clapped his hands together.

The German seemed so elated that Norman rather hated to dampen his moment of triumph. Still, Occam's razor and simple common sense obliged him to speak. "It's likely," he said, "that we simply didn't get the table leveled properly. Or else the scale slipped out of adjustment."

"Then we'll check both," Schmidt replied, "and weigh again."

They did. The reading was the same as before. The physicist brought out a tape measure and used it to define the scale's position in relation to fixed reference points in the room.

As he held his end of the tape, Norman felt lightheaded. Could the variance possibly be real?

One obvious alternative was that, at some point in his life, Schmidt had acquired the skills of a prestidigitator and was using them to perpetrate a hoax, possibly switching one weight for another. But Norman could not imagine why a scientist with a first-rate reputation and bright future to protect would stoop to such a fraud, nor did the notion jibe with his sense of the young man's character.

No matter how carefully the two scientists leveled the table and checked the scale—and how keenly Norman watched Schmidt, just in case the latter was attempting chicanery after all—the next several placements yielded similarly anomalous results. Gradually a pattern, a gradient, emerged. Objects became ever so slightly lighter, which meant gravity became marginally weaker, as one approached the icebox in the corner of the kitchen.

As he helped shift the table and held his end of the measuring tape, Norman's initial stupefaction gave way to an excitement akin to Schmidt's. He was no nearer to solving his own scientific puzzle, but he was not quite so fixated on it as to render him indifferent to someone else's amazing discovery, nor was it lost on him that his participation, even in a secondary role, might redeem his colleagues' disdainful opinion of him.

Gradually, though, as he and Schmidt shifted the table progressively closer to the icebox, his emotions altered once again. His interest remained, but a growing uneasiness undercut it. Eventually, like an image coming clear when one focused a telescope, the anxiety resolved itself into the suspicion that he and the German were being observed.

As they were. When he glanced around, Mrs. Page was viewing the work with an expression that proclaimed her conviction that her visitors were out of their minds.

Clearly, her scrutiny must be the source of Norman's edginess, but to his annoyance, realizing that did not banish the feeling. His mouth remained dry, and a clumsy tightness persisted in his limbs.

The moment came when the table was flush with the icebox and the final weight recorded. Schmidt reached into the corner.

Norman wanted to shout, *Don't!* But he didn't want to appear ridiculous, so he remained silent.

Schmidt felt around the space where one wall met the other. Unlike the weighings, nothing about the manner in which his fingertips tapped the faded wallpaper was peculiar. Still, Norman's sense of being observed intensified, and although he assured himself it was just some fleeting, meaningless agitation of the nerves, he nonetheless felt relieved when Schmidt drew back his hand.

They restored the table to its original position, and Schmidt repacked the valise. Giving Mrs. Page a smile, he said, "Thank you for your patience. Should it prove necessary, may we call again?"

She shrugged. "If you keep making it worth my while."

= **4** =

After returning the valise to the Bearcat's trunk, Schmidt clapped Norman on the back. "The first house we checked!" he exclaimed. "The very first!"

"What we found was remarkable," Norman replied. "That is, assuming there isn't another explanation, and the observations can be replicated."

Schmidt waved the comment away. "They will be."

"If so," said Norman, "unexplainable fluctuations in gravity are an extraordinary discovery. But we *didn't* find a discontinuity in space-time."

"True. We're not hitting on all six yet. But what a start!" The physicist extracted a silver case from a pocket of the Lindbergh jacket and offered a celebratory cigarette to Norman. Hoping for some exotic European flavor, the American was a bit disappointed that the tobacco tasted pretty much the same as the Chesterfields that were his accustomed brand.

Exhaling smoke, he said, "Do you have any thoughts as to why no discontinuity was in evidence?"

"At this point," Schmidt replied, "we know so little that any speculation is little more than guesswork. But, that said, what if the discontinuity was unstable? The unfortunate patriots disappeared all the way back in 1774. That gave the breach a century-and-a-half to close. Or shrink to microscopic size."

"Maybe. If the discontinuities come and go, that would explain how people like the Pages can live in the same places where others disappeared and never notice anything odd."

"It also raises the possibility that there may not be any open breaches left in Arkham. But I refuse to be pessimistic after such a promising beginning! I prefer to believe that if we simply work our way down the list, we'll find one. Let's get a wiggle on!"

= 5 =

The scientists' next stop was South Church itself, or rather, the small graveyard adjacent to it. As they began their work, a priest who introduced himself as Father Michael arrived to ask what they were doing but, invoking his status as a professor at Miskatonic, Norman satisfied the man as to their bona fides.

Unfortunately, the outdoor site posed longer-lasting hindrances, such as the lack of Mrs. Page's dining room table and the floor on which it sat. Schmidt's valise proved to contain a folding table with stubby telescoping legs that was just big enough to hold the balance scale, but it was less convenient to keep bending over it and more difficult to level it on the ground.

The greatest hindrance, however, was that while the accounts that had drawn Schmidt to this location indicated that three people had vanished—a sexton digging a grave in 1845, a widow come to put roses on her husband's final resting place in 1889, and a pair of truant schoolboys as recently as 1909—they did not indicate where in the cemetery the disappearances had occurred. Thus, it was necessary to perform exploratory weighings all around the rectangular space within the waist-high fieldstone walls.

As the two men labored among crumbling tombstones and ivy-covered mausoleums, gray clouds smothered the sun, threatened rain, and brought a hint of autumn chill. Still, Schmidt worked on with cheerful enthusiasm. Something, pride perhaps, compelled Norman to try to match the younger man's energy even when his lower back began to ache.

Eventually they made their way to the northeastern quadrant of the graveyard. As he slipped cardboard under a table leg, Norman abruptly felt a renewed suspicion of scrutiny. With it came another pang of trepidation, even though the feeling of being spied upon was plainly more baseless than before. Mrs. Page was not here, and Father Michael had gone back inside the church.

Schmidt set the weight on the scale. "Voilà! Only this time, the weight is heavier instead of lighter."

Norman tried to keep any irrational anxiety out of his voice. "What do you make of that?"

"I have no idea, but it's interesting. Now we have to figure out where the trail of anomalies leads from here."

Norman hesitated, then shoved away the pusillanimous urge. He pointed to the spot where the low cemetery wall took a right-angle bend. "We should try that direction first."

Schmidt cocked his head. "Why?"

"In Mrs. Page's apartment, the gradient led to a corner."

"It's difficult to imagine that's any more than a coincidence, but I don't have a better suggestion. So why not?"

It soon became apparent that Norman's hunch was correct. Schmidt whooped and gave him another clap on the shoulder.

As before, the gravitational disturbances spread out in a fan shape from a presumed point of origin. Only this time, in place of a steady gradient, the weight was too heavy in one spot, too light at the next, and too heavy again at the third.

His heart thumping, Norman conjectured the difference reflected the fact that the previous discontinuity had opened in 1774 and this one as recently as 1909. Perhaps when they did, they created gravitational chaos, and after they closed, the anomalies settled toward a more orderly resting state.

But that was not how the situation *felt*. Crazy though it was, his imagination suggested that gravity was more disturbed than before because the invisible watcher was staring more intently. Or more *maliciously*. He wondered if he and Schmidt were like prey obliviously approaching a hungry tiger hidden in tall grass.

He reached to pick up the scale and nearly knocked it over. "Are you all right?" asked Schmidt.

Norman swallowed. "Fine."

"Are you sure? Your hands are trembling,"

Norman forced a smile. "I'm not as young as you, but I'm not going to fall over dead, either. Not and miss out on all the excitement."

Had he been candid about it, he would have said he was not going to disgrace himself by succumbing to groundless fear. He did not know what ailed him—maybe he would see his doctor when he had the chance—but he was a scientist, and he was going to behave as such.

They reached the juncture of the two walls. Schmidt waved his hands through the air above. Norman held his breath, and…nothing happened.

Schmidt dropped to one knee and Norman's anxiety ratcheted up another notch. He had to struggle not to wince despite himself as his thoughts returned to the crouching tiger he had imagined previously. No such beast was present—obviously—but if one entertained the fantasy that it was, Schmidt had just put himself eye to eye with it.

The physicist felt around the gray, fitted fieldstone, and the corner proved to be as solid as it looked. No hitherto undetected hole in the substance of things yawned in response to the probing.

Schmidt rose and brushed off his pant leg. "Do you want to try?"

"No!" Norman yelped. He took a breath. "I mean, I don't see a point. You were thorough. I wouldn't do anything you didn't mere moments before."

"Suit yourself. I just don't want to hog the fun." Thunder rumbled, and a first raindrop plopped on Norman's shoulder. "Let's pack up and get some supper. My treat, and I insist on somewhere expensive."

As they walked toward the cemetery gate, Norman's sense of being watched faded, as did the anxiety that accompanied it. He resolved that he would not succumb to such idiocy again. Or permit himself to harbor the suspicion that he and Schmidt had now been lucky twice.

═ 6 ═

Paneled in dark oak with frosted Art Nouveau wall fixtures providing soft illumination, Drew's was one of Uptown's better restaurants. Once, Norman had been a regular. After he witnessed the six stars vanishing, though, a visit to any such establishment came to feel like a waste of time better spent in his study. Now, dining on shepherd's pie, he rather felt he had been cheating himself.

The unavailability of wine or beer to accompany one's meal had provoked Schmidt into a humorous lamentation on the puritanical American character and the absurdity of Prohibition, but now that the food had arrived, he did not appear to miss alcohol all that much. He was attacking his broiled Boston scrod with the gusto he brought to everything in life.

Norman sipped his coffee. "It's good, isn't it?"

"It's the elephant's eyebrows," the German replied, "and there's nothing like discovering something to give a scientist an appetite."

Norman grunted. "I suppose."

"What's eating you, partner? Most of the time, you seem as excited as I am, but every once in a while, you turn into a bit of a wurp."

Norman's immediate impulse was to deny it. Then, however, it occurred to him that he could in some measure acknowledge his edginess without mentioning imaginary watchers or admitting to irrational anxiety attacks.

"I just wonder," he said, "if you're being a little reckless."

Schmidt cocked his head. "How so?"

"Your hypothesis is that the discontinuities exist and people occasionally blunder through them never to be seen again, and there you are groping around for them with your bare hands. What if *you* fall in?"

The physicist grinned. "Then I'll have the most glorious adventure any scientist ever had."

"I'm serious."

"So am I. Well, in principle, but in practice, perhaps you raise a valid point. Suppose I do the initial probing with a stick. Will that make you feel better?"

"Yes." A little, anyway.

"Then that's how we'll do it." Schmidt pushed his plate away, dabbed at his lips with his napkin, and set it on the table. "Are you game for one more site before we seek out one of these juice joints I've heard so much about?"

Norman frowned. "It's dark, and it's raining."

"I'm sure we can find flashlights and umbrellas, and we'll choose another indoor location. Come on, what do you say?"

Norman reminded himself that he had resolved to put irrational anxiety behind him. "All right. One more."

= 7 =

The farm—if it still was a working farm—lay beyond the city limits of Arkham, on a narrow unpaved road that twisted west from the Aylesbury Pike. The land near the road was overgrown, and no lights shined in the house in the distance. If not for the flashes of lightning, Norman might have missed seeing the vague black mass of it and the larger shape that was the barn.

A chain hung across the drive with a tin *No Trespassing* sign wired to the middle of it. The wind tugged at their umbrellas as he and Schmidt shined their tungsten-filament flashlights on the sign. The chain was not rusty, and weather had yet to fade or stain the lettering.

That felt incongruous, but Norman supposed it shouldn't, really. Whether or not anyone was farming the land, someone presumably still owned it.

"It's a good thing the equipment weighs no more than it does," said Schmidt. "We can ankle the rest of the way."

Norman frowned. "The sign says—"

"Oh, come on! We're not going to hurt anything. No one will even know we were here." He grinned. "For science!"

Norman returned a grudging smile. "Very well. For science."

He opened the trunk, and Schmidt took out the valise. Norman gave the Bearcat a last look, decided no harm would come to it parked where it was on the side of the lonely road, and followed his companion as the German stepped over the chain and headed up the drive.

The wind gusted, and cold rain slipped beneath his umbrella to spatter him. The brush rustled and swayed as though animals were moving through it, although only blackness showed in the gaps between branches. Norman resisted the urge to play his flashlight beam across the overgrowth just to make sure.

"Do we want the house or the barn?"

"The barn," Schmidt replied. "In 1871, a farmer went in and

never came out. In 1910, virtually the same thing happened again, this time to the missing man's eldest son."

Up close, the farmhouse and barn looked as abandoned as before. The barn had big doors on the front where wagons, traction engines, and such had presumably gone in and out. Schmidt ignored the large doors in favor of a smaller entrance around the side. He tried the knob, and the door opened.

The dark space inside still smelled of hay, but it was not open and empty the way Norman expected. As he and Schmidt stepped inside, the flashlights' circles of glow flowed across stacks of wooden crates on pallets. He was still trying to figure out exactly what they had stumbled across when a baritone voice barked, "Don't move!"

Norman turned toward the sound. A square-jawed young man in his shirtsleeves and braces was aiming a pistol at the intruders. Behind him, too far away for Norman to have noticed its light from outside, a hurricane lantern sat on a small table where it illuminated a pack of Lucky Strikes, an overflowing ashtray, and a facedown issue of *Western Stories Weekly*.

"Don't shoot!" Norman exclaimed. It was all he could think of to say.

The gunman peered at them. "You don't look like cops. Or hijackers, neither."

"We're scientists," Norman said, his pulse beating in his neck. "I'm Professor Norman from Miskatonic, and this is Professor Schmidt from the University of Berlin. We came here for purposes of research. We thought the property was abandoned."

"Well, it ain't," the guard replied. "And Old Sadie Sheldon don't like others sniffin' around his properties." According to the *Arkham Advertiser*, Sheldon was a bootlegger, so the crates presumably held Canadian whiskey. "And now that you've seen that, what the hell am I supposed to do with you?"

"Nothing?" Norman ventured.

"Oh, yeah? How does *that* work?"

"Why would we talk to the police?" Norman asked. "We enjoy a drink the same as anybody else, whereas we *don't* care for the prospect of experiencing whatever it is that Mr. Sheldon does to informers."

The gangster grunted. "Okay, that's smart. Scram. And

remember, you told me your names."

Schmidt cleared his throat. "Actually, now that we're here, may we proceed with our investigation? We won't disturb the merchandise or do anything that would draw attention."

The bootlegger frowned. "I don't know much about science, but ain't the whole idea to tell people what you figure out?"

"Yes," Norman said, "but we might not find anything in this particular location. We may just check it and cross it off our list. If we *do* discover something of interest, we'll still say nothing without Mr. Sheldon's approval. You have my word."

The guard stood and pondered while scratching his cheek with the muzzle of his automatic. Finally he said, "Go on, then. But don't take all night, and leave the brown alone. I'll be keeping an eye on you."

"Thank you," Schmidt said, and then, in a softer voice, as he set down the valise, "Nice work double shuffling him, old boy. I didn't know you had it in you."

Norman smiled. "Maybe your bad example is rubbing off on me. I take it we're following the usual procedure?"

"Actually," said Schmidt, "I hope to find a shortcut. The disappearance of Zachariah Mayhew—the son—differed from the others we've investigated in one respect. He left behind a pool of blood on the floor."

The satisfaction Norman had felt at persuading the hoodlum, and at Schmidt's approval, gave way to a fresh pang of trepidation. Annoyed with himself and trying to resist the resurgence of his timidity, he said, "Then we look for a stain. If we find one, that's the right area in which to start recording weights."

"Exactly," Schmidt replied.

Shining his flashlight on the floor, Norman headed down one of the aisles between the stacks of liquor crates. The edginess was trying to worm its way back into his head and he felt an urge to hurry, to be done with this task and away, but he made himself go slowly anyway. With the boxes blocking the yellow glow of the guard's lantern, the barn was even darker than before. The bloodstain, if still present at all, was likely to be faded and difficult to distinguish from the general dust and grime. If he did not proceed carefully, he might very well miss it.

From time to time, a shadow with a single luminous eye

appeared at the end of an aisle to make him flinch and squint at the glare. It was the hoodlum, prowling with lantern in hand to make sure the scientists were not opening any of the whiskey crates. The bootlegger did not appear very often, however. Apparently, he had decided his uninvited guests truly were harmless, and he was enjoying the stories in his cowboy pulp.

Somewhat more frequently, a band of rain fell hard enough to rattle on the roof, or the wind gusted hard enough to make the old barn groan and creak. The former sounded like claws tapping. Rats—or something bigger than rats—scuttled nearby but out of sight. The latter made Norman imagine the unknown force of Schmidt's hypothesis pulling apart the juncture of two walls to reveal a gash in the flesh of the world itself.

Idiocy. Norman had to get hold of himself. He halted and took several deep breaths. His heartbeat slowed, and some of the tension shivered out of his limbs. Then someone screamed.

Norman recognized the voice, although the wordless cry of terror was unlike anything he had heard it produce hitherto. "Schmidt?" he called.

"Run!" the physicist wailed. The next instant, he shrieked again.

"What the hell!" the bootlegger shouted. With that, he was presumably up and moving to discover the reason for the disturbance.

Norman yearned to do as Schmidt had bade him and flee, but he couldn't just abandon the German. Resisting the lure of possible escape as if it, too, were some sort of gravitational anomaly, he managed to take a step in a different direction, and then another after that.

Due to the way sound echoed beneath the high roof and through the aisles of crates, he hadn't been able to tell exactly where Schmidt's cries originated, but he suspected it was somewhere near one of the far corners of the barn. Breathing in short little rasps, he crept toward the closer of the two. The pattering he'd heard before returned and now seemed to move with him, as though the phantom rat pack he'd imagined previously was stalking him.

Amber light pushed at the gloom ahead. The guard stepped into the intersection of Norman's aisle with his automatic leveled and his lantern held high.

Norman drew breath to call out to the other man, but before he could, the guard let out a yelp. His eyes wide, he stretched out his shooting arm and fired three times.

A moment later, he lowered the automatic, and Norman's shoulders slumped in relief. The bootlegger's behavior seemed to indicate the gunfire had killed the source of his cries or had at least alarmed it into retreat.

Then wood crashed, and glass shattered. Startled, Norman peered about in an effort to find the source of the new disturbance. The bootlegger did the same, then hastily backpedaled out of sight. As he disappeared, he raised his pistol and fired upward.

Ahead of Norman and to his right, stacks of crates swayed. Dark shapes leaped to the stacks on the left in what seemed to be a pursuit of the gunman. The forms were sufficiently high above Norman's flashlight beam and departed so quickly that his eyes registered nothing more than a surge of movement. But their mass and the vigor of their springing dislodged the upper boxes, and the crates smashed to the floor.

More shots rang out. Additional crates fell. Silence followed. Norman crept up to the intersection and peered around the corner.

There was nothing to see but a splash of light where the bootlegger had tried to retreat down a different aisle. The glow wasn't dimming however, which meant both the lantern, and the man who carried it, had stopped moving. Norman imagined the man lying torn and dead with *something* crouching over him.

Surely poor Schmidt had been the first to die. Norman would be crazy to linger in this place a moment longer. Worried fear would make him clumsy, *noisy,* he gathered himself to sneak toward the exit. Then the physicist resumed his shrieking.

Convinced that whatever had killed the bootlegger would rush to silence Schmidt's cries, and in so doing charge within arm's reach of him, Norman flattened himself against the wall of crates. The cringing, reflexive action produced a thump, and the stack above him began to rock and sway, making his discovery seem all the more likely.

But nothing came. Maybe the *things* were too eager to eat the bootlegger to react to Schmidt's screams or, in this isolated location with rain falling, wind blowing, and thunder booming outside, didn't regard the racket as cause for concern.

Whatever the explanation, Schmidt was still alive, and perhaps Norman could help him to safety without the *things* being any the wiser. At least the ongoing cries now revealed the German's approximate location. It was near one of the corners of the barn, precisely where Norman's colleague had expected to find the source of the anomalies.

With the smells of gun smoke and spilled whiskey now hanging in the air, Norman skulked across the intersection. *Just get there*, he told himself, *just get there. It's only a few more steps.*

That was true, but unfortunately, the walls of crates would make it impossible to catch even a glimpse of what awaited until he was quite close indeed. As he approached the end of an aisle, vapor, invisible except for where it tainted the white beam of the flashlight, swirled through the air. For an instant, he imagined it was smoke, but he didn't know what would have started a fire. The hoodlum and his hurricane lantern were behind him, not ahead.

An instant later, he caught a whiff of the vapor and all but gagged in revulsion. The stench was also suggestive of smoke in that it called to mind the incineration of a rotting corpse. Norman had never smelled such a thing, but had he attempted to imagine it, he might have hit on something foul and acrid like this.

Holding his breath, he peeked around the end of the stacks of crates and spied Schmidt at last.

Or rather, Norman spied most of him.

Still screaming despite growing hoarse and short of breath, Schmidt lay on his belly in the corner with his upper body pointed outward. His hands clutched and scrabbled at the floor. From points midway down the calves, his legs were simply absent, as if sticking out a hole in the wall of the barn. But there was no such opening, merely denser twists of the malodorous fog.

Schmidt hitched backward, gradually losing the struggle to anchor himself as *something* pulled him into nothingness. Breaking cover, Norman dashed forward to grab his colleague's hand and haul him free.

As though Schmidt's unseen captor had been only toying with him hitherto—or as if it had waited for Norman's arrival to tease and frustrate *him*—the German's body shot backward faster than the older man could close the distance. The corner swallowed

Schmidt's torso, head, arms, clawing hands, and then nothing at all remained.

$$= \quad 8 \quad =$$

Off balance as he was, Norman couldn't stop in time to avoid banging into the juncture of the two walls. The impact jolted him and bounced him reeling backward, as a collision with solid matter should.

He stepped forward again and, hands shaking, stooped to examine the base of the walls, which was to say, the exact spot through which Schmidt had disappeared. It was as solid as the walls that surrounded it.

An instant later, a sense of malevolent attention pierced him through. As though, having dealt with Schmidt to its satisfaction, the physicist's abductor had swung its head back toward the camouflage behind which it hid like a trapdoor spider. Then it howled.

Partly, the cry hurt Norman's ears as any loud noise would. But there was also a component of it that seemed to rip directly into the mind itself.

Other howls answered. The *things* still in the barn were signaling their readiness to deal with him. He bolted.

After several strides, he realized his flashlight was likely to help his pursuers find him. Fumbling, he clicked it off and could see nothing. He continued in what he thought was the right direction and banged face first into what must be a stack of crates. He gasped, less at the jolt of pain than at the telltale noise.

Blundering onward, he ran the fingertips of one hand over the rough wood of the crates. It helped him avoid another collision but *didn't* avert the moment when a panicky sense of disorientation suddenly overwhelmed him. Exactly where was he in the barn? Was he still moving toward an exit? And where were the creatures? Their howling was hideous, terrifying, but at least it had provided some vague sense of their location. Now he could hear nothing but the clatter of rain on the roof.

His fingers slipped from splintery wood to empty air. He'd reached the end of a wall of crates. He groped forward and pushed against a barrier. Believing it to be a barn wall, he started to turn away, then realized it had given ever so slightly under the pressure of his hands.

He reached lower and found a bar in brackets. He'd blundered his way to the big double doors and, thank the Lord, only this simple mechanism secured them. He was going to get away!

He grabbed hold of the bar, shoved it, and it stuck. Either it, the brackets, or both were warped and swollen.

The creatures howled anew. They had spotted him, and they were coming.

Screaming, he pushed with all his might, and, scraping and squealing, the bar slid sideways. He threw himself at the door on the left, knocked it open, stumbled through, and sprinted toward the road.

Every instant of the way, he expected a *thing* to overtake him and rip him apart, or drag him shrieking through a hole in the world. It was only when he had the Bearcat speeding as fast as the sixteen-valve, four cylinder engine could manage that he decided that, for whatever reason, the creatures had abandoned the chase. Then tears blurred the darkened road and the lights of Arkham ahead. He pulled over and broke down sobbing.

═ 9 ═

Seated across the table from Norman, the pages of the astronomer's typed and signed statement lying between them, Sheriff Engle took another drink of coffee. As Norman had previously discovered, the stuff tasted awful, but with his bloodshot eyes, puffy lids, and unshaven jowls, the lawman looked like he needed it, and that was understandable. Some subordinate had woken him in the middle of the night to report that one of the professors from the university had turned up raving about a vanished German, a harrowing chase, and the Lord only knew what else.

In truth, Norman lived and worked in Arkham and had automatically run to the Arkham Police Department in Easttown. There, however, the man on the night desk, one Officer Galeas, determined the "incident" had occurred beyond the city limits and, radiating a certain mischievous relish, handed him off to the Sheriff's Department, who conveniently shared the same building.

Lanky, with a thatch of straw-colored hair, Deputy Dingby looked as dyspeptic as his superior and with an arguably better reason: the sheriff had tasked him with visiting the barn where Schmidt had disappeared. As a result, he was now as rain-soaked and disheveled as he was tired.

"Well," the sheriff said, addressing Norman, "you've had some time to think." He didn't add *or sober up,* but Norman suspected the latter possibility was in his thoughts. "Do you want to change your story?"

"No," Norman answered. In retrospect, it should have been obvious that his account was unbelievable. But when a man was abducted before one's eyes, by whatever and to wherever, what was there to do but report it to the authorities?

"You sure?" the sheriff persisted. "Because I can imagine it happening this way. You and this German fella drank some bad coffin varnish and went a little crazy. Started seeing things. He got scared and ran off through the fields. Once he comes to his senses, he'll likely turn up. If not, we can track him down in the daylight."

Norman shook his head. "It all happened just the way I told you."

"With holes in the world."

"Yes."

"And monsters."

"Yes."

"Although you didn't really ever see either of those things."

Norman hesitated. "I saw Professor Schmidt slide through the discontinuity. Apparently a person can't see the breach itself."

"You saw him go through. But when you felt around the spot just a second later, the walls were solid."

"Yes. Still, there has to be some kind of evidence." Norman turned to Deputy Dingby. "You searched. What did you find?"

Sheriff Engle waved a hand in a gesture of acquiescence. "Sure, why not? Run it down for us, Deputy."

"Well," the deputy said, "the black case with the scale and such was there. So were umbrellas, flashlights, a lantern, a pulp cowboy magazine, and all that whiskey, some of the crates fallen and broken open." He smiled a crooked smile. "The Prohibition Agents are going to be happy."

The sheriff made a spitting sound. "That's wonderful, Deputy. I live to make the prohis happy. But what's important here and now is that we can be fairly sure the two professors really were there like our witness claims. Maybe the bootlegger guard, too. Now let's hear the things you *didn't* find. My guess is that bodies are at the top of the list."

The deputy took a breath. "That's right, sir. There were no bodies."

"There wouldn't have been," Norman said, "if the creatures dragged them back through the breaches."

"Any big pools and splashes of blood," the sheriff asked, "where it looked like somebody got mauled? Like by a bear or a rabid dog or something?"

Deputy Dingby swallowed. "No."

"What about the mysterious holes? Did you tap around in the corners like I told you to?"

"Yes, sir. Everything was solid."

The sheriff looked at Norman and spread his hands palms up. "There you have it."

Norman fixed his gaze on the deputy. "When Sheriff Engle asked about bodies, you hesitated. When he asked about pools of blood, you did it again. I don't accuse you of lying outright, but I believe you held back *something.*"

The deputy hesitated once more, obviously torn between the inclination to be honest and the desire to please his boss by helping to speed the importunate crackpot academic on his way.

Sheriff Engle heaved a sigh. "Deputy, if you found *anything* funny, lay it out for us."

"Yes, sir," he replied. He reached into the pocket of his brown uniform trousers, brought out a folded handkerchief, unwrapped the contents, and set the object on the table between the two men. It was a fingernail with a trace of dried blood encrusting the bottom.

"You found it on the floor," Norman said, "in the southwest corner of the barn."

The deputy frowned. "Yeah."

Norman turned back to the sheriff. "This proves what I told you! It's Schmidt's fingernail! It tore loose when he was clutching at the floor and the beast was dragging him backward!"

"Come on, Professor. You're supposed to be a scientist. You know damn well it isn't proof of anything."

"It…" Norman faltered. It was maddening that the sheriff still doubted, but he made a valid point. By itself, the fingernail *wasn't* enough to demonstrate the truth of the story. "Look. You know Professor Schmidt was with me in the barn. You know he's gone now. What's *your* explanation?"

"You already heard it."

"He wandered off in an alcohol-induced delirium."

"If you don't like that story, I can think of others."

Norman felt a pang of trepidation. "Meaning what, exactly?"

"If you two just got pie-eyed, that's not so bad. Plenty of people drink, the Volstead Act be damned. But you don't look lathered now, and you're still telling the same story, so maybe that was never really the problem. Maybe you're crackers."

"That's ridiculous."

"Is it? I made a couple calls, woke up a couple people from the university. Apparently you have a reputation for being strange. Maybe you're strange enough that I should check you into the asylum for observation."

"There are no grounds! You wouldn't dare!"

"I might. I might also *dare* to consider you a suspect if your German friend doesn't turn up. From what I understand, you were pretty damn eager to drive him around. And you were the last person to see him before he disappeared. A young fella already at the top of his profession when you're getting on in years and something of a joke…" Sheriff Engle shrugged. "Who could blame you for being jealous?"

"So I murdered him and then came straight to you with a wild story you were all too likely to disbelieve?"

"If you're insane, maybe you didn't realize just how unbelievable it was. You thought you were giving yourself an alibi."

Norman looked the sheriff in the eye. "Whatever else you believe or don't believe, you don't really think I killed Professor Schmidt or need to be institutionalized. Why are you trying to intimidate me into retracting my story?"

"Maybe I'm trying to protect you from what everyone else is likely to think."

"I'm not asking you to do that."

The sheriff settled back in his chair. "Okay, then let me tell you about a sheriff's job. Mostly, it's what you expect. If there's a thief stealing people's chickens, I catch him. If a landlord evicts a tenant who then refuses to leave, I boot him out. Straightforward problems with straightforward answers."

Norman scowled. "How is this relevant?"

"Bear with me. I'm getting there. Once in a while, though, something comes up that's bad or scary and *doesn't* have an easy answer. In those situations, maybe the best a sheriff can do is keep a lid on what's really happening. That way, people don't panic."

"Are you saying you *do* believe me?"

Sheriff Engle shook his head. "Don't flatter yourself. But I know funny things happen once in a while, and I've been doing this job long enough to wonder if they don't happen more often around here than in some other places. Anyway, what it all comes down to is this: My men and I will look for Professor Schmidt the same way we'd look for any missing person, but we're not going to act like men from Mars kidnapped him or whatever it is you think happened. Because even if that was true, what the hell could we do about it?"

Norman's emotions—the urgency, the anger—crumpled into a kind of exhausted resignation. "What exactly do you want me to do?"

"First, forget you ever said this bullshit." The sheriff picked up the pages of the statement and tore them in two. "Then give me something that will enable me to declare Schmidt missing and start a search without making it look like we're both out of our minds. You were helping him do research. You don't know what the point was because he's a physicist and you're an astronomer. He wanted to go to the farm, so you took him. The whiskey was there, but you didn't see a bootlegger or anybody like that. You wandered off from Schmidt to take a look around the barn. When you came back he was gone. And that's all you know."

"Got it," Norman said.

10

As soon as he entered the classroom, Norman decided he had made a mistake.

Given his ordeal, and the hours with the Sheriff's Department that followed, lack of sleep alone would have provided him with a more than adequate excuse for taking the day off. But he knew he would not be able to rest, and the presence of others and the resumption of routine seemed as if they might protect him from the shuddering fits that could otherwise afflict him.

The problem, though, was that every seat was filled, with more students standing along the back wall. In many cases, they were young men and women whose faces Norman had never seen before. Plainly, the majority of those present had come to gawk at the Science Department's resident eccentric, now more than ever an object of curiosity by dint of his involvement in a celebrated colleague's disappearance.

Well, damn them all. This was an astronomy class, not a circus sideshow. To spite them, he launched into his discourse on Neptune, and Lowell's unsuccessful search for planets beyond, more forcefully than he had delivered any lecture in years.

Unfortunately, neither his energy nor the intrinsic interest of his subject matter sufficed to divert his audience's curiosity into the appropriate channels. When he turned his back to write on the blackboard, they whispered back and forth. The chatter was too soft for him to make out, but he did catch "nuts," "crazy," "did *something*," and "involved *somehow*."

No doubt it would have been far worse had Sheriff Engle permitted his original statement to stand. As it was, the speculation and suspicion might fade in time. Still, teeth gritted, Norman bore down until the chalk snapped in two.

He stretched out the lecture without acknowledging any of the waving hands that sought to interrupt him. Someone might want to ask a question that actually pertained to astronomy, but he was unwilling to chance it. The instant the bell rang, he slammed the textbook shut, snatched it off the lectern, and rushed for the door.

Sadly, his haste merely served to fling him into the clutches of a smiling, apple-cheeked man in a polka-dot bow tie and homburg. Absurdly, a press pass stuck up from the hatband as though Arkham were a major city like Boston or New York.

"Professor Withers," the journalist said, "a moment of your time?"

"Sorry," Norman said, circling around the man, "I'm in a hurry."

The newspaperman scrambled to catch up and fell into step

beside him. "Come on, Professor, be a sport. I'm Doyle Jeffries. I *edit* the Advertiser, and I came down here personally just to hear what you've got to say."

"Nothing. It's all in the information the sheriff already released."

"You sure? It seemed to me there were lots of holes in that story."

"It's everything I know. Please excuse me." Norman quickened his pace, and this time Doyle allowed him to escape.

He stamped onward into the Science Department offices, ignoring the stares and awkward greetings of secretaries and the other faculty. He entered his own cramped little sanctuary, with its overflowing bookshelves, stacks of journals, star charts and examples of astrophotography, and slammed the door. Copious torn-paper bookmarks and Moore Push-Pins indicated the locations of data he had, at one time or another, believed might shed light on the puzzle that had consumed the past decade of his life.

Two new items reposed front and center on his crowded desk. One was a note informing him the Dean wanted to see him. Yesterday, Norman, cranky recluse that he knew himself to be, would have responded expeditiously. But currently, it simply was not in him.

The second item was the new issue of *The Astronomical Journal*. He opened it and, as was his habit, set out to read it cover to cover.

He had spent countless hours engaged in such study, yet now, for the first time since adjusting to the finalization of his divorce, he had difficulty concentrating. He perused paragraphs or whole pages only to realize he had retained none of the information. The image of Schmidt wailing, scrabbling in vain for handholds, and vanishing kept appearing before his inner eye.

But that was not the only thing distracting him. The office itself was not alarming, and his instincts did not warn of some invisible predator poised to spring. But the space seemed dusty and dingy. Oppressive to the point of claustrophobia. The odd thought came to him that if he heard of a convict sentenced to years of solitary confinement in a cell like this, he would feel sorry for the man.

Still, it was more tolerable than being stared at. He stayed where he was until he heard the sounds of the rest of the department going home for the day, and for some time thereafter. When his pocket watch informed him night had fallen, he emerged from his hiding place and skulked from the Science building onto the quad. A few people were wandering around in the dark, but no one noticed him as he headed for the Administration building, at the top of which was his telescope.

He entered to find the place empty of administrative staff, custodians, and anyone else for that matter, which was just as well.

Norman threw himself into the process of operating the telescope. Here, behind the lens, was where he truly belonged. This was what his life was all about, not the nightmare Schmidt had led him into. If he immersed himself in it anew, surely he could purge himself of the emotions tearing at his insides.

His preparations complete, he pressed his eye to the eyepiece. The portion of the sky that was his abiding preoccupation appeared, looking as it had always looked through years of repeated viewings. The six vanished stars had not returned. There was nothing to provide a clue as to what had become of them. God had not parted the black, spangled curtain of the firmament to expound on the question.

Norman felt a sudden urge to pound on the telescope with his fists. He did not succumb to it, but he stepped away from the instrument for fear that he would. He was breathing heavily, and his chest and arms felt tight.

Over the years, he had often been keenly aware others viewed him as a laughable or pathetic figure. He had told himself that when he finally made his great discovery, they would amend their opinions. Now it came to him that, doing the same things day after day and night, it was all but certain he never would solve the mystery. It also struck him that even if, by some extraordinary stroke of fortune, he did, his life would *still* look pitiful and in large measure misspent. Somehow, that thought was the worst of all.

He assured himself it was merely fear provoking such dismal notions. Once he calmed down, his chosen path would seem as worthwhile as it always had.

But truly, anxiety was not the problem. He was still afraid. For an aging academic who had never before faced any sort of danger, it could scarcely be otherwise. Yet, the occasional stab of dread notwithstanding, now that he had put miles and hours between himself and the barn, he actually felt more safe than not.

No, when he took inventory of his tangled emotions, it came to him that his current wretchedness stemmed less from residual fear than from shame. He felt guilty that he had acquiesced to Sheriff Engle's decision to suppress the truth, and guiltier still about what had happened to Schmidt.

Idiocy! If there was anything he should have learned from the way his life had unfolded, it was the folly of espousing a truth no one would believe. He clearly wasn't to blame for the physicist's fate. He'd *tried* to rescue Schmidt but had simply been no match for the *thing* that took him.

True. But he was not trying anymore, was he?

More idiocy! Schmidt was surely dead.

Well, no, not *surely*. Norman lacked evidence to confirm any such conclusion. He did not know why the German had been taken. If the breaches were a manifestation of twisted space-time, he could not even know how much subjective time had passed for Schmidt since his captor yanked him through. Perhaps it had only been an instant.

Which, although an interesting speculation, shed no light whatsoever on how to go about retrieving him. Norman hauled the long-legged chair out from under the telescope, lit a Chesterfield, and climbed up into the seat to ponder what he knew.

He quickly decided that was almost nothing. Schmidt had come looking for holes in ordinary reality and, tragically, found them. But nothing in the physicist's rudimentary hypothesis explained why the breaches seemed to occur only in the corners of man-made structures, why they opened and closed like doors at the behest of creatures lurking on the other side, or what those entities were. A man would have to understand such things to have *any* hope of rescuing someone who had been taken, and Norman had no idea where to look for the requisite information.

Or did he? He still had the list of locations Schmidt had given him at the start of their time together. The majority remained to be explored, although the prospect of doing so made a chill slide up his spine.

Intuition told him he had somehow escaped the *things*. Was he really contemplating offering them another crack at him? What had befallen Schmidt was horrible, but it was not his responsibility to fix it. He had his own life to think about.

Except that he had already examined that life and found it wanting, certainly when compared to that of a brilliant, exuberant young man with many years of "glorious adventure" still before him. If unclouded by fear or selfishness, any rational mind would put a bitter old failure like Norman at hazard if there was the slightest chance of winning the German back thereby. Indeed, he had a sense that turning away would be tantamount to throwing away the final chance for his own life to mean something.

Dear Lord, he thought, astonished by his own audacity, *I'm going to do it*. He opened his notebook and wrote a note explaining he was taking a leave of absence. For the moment, the dean could be content with that.

Part Two
The House of Powder Mill Street

$=$ **11** $=$

Somewhat to Norman's dismay, it proved impossible to find a parking spot right in front of the offices of the *Arkham Advertiser*. He had to pull up to the curb outside a gray box of a shoe factory a block away. Norman climbed out of the Bearcat feeling somewhat like a man condemned to run the gantlet.

But to his relief, in contrast to the unwelcome attention he had attracted at the university, no one on the street looked twice at him. With its factories, warehouses, and tenements with clotheslines hanging above the alleys that sliced between them, Northside was too busy with commerce to take note of a stray academic. Even one linked to a mysterious disappearance. Besides, Schmidt likely did not seem like such a celebrity hereabouts as he did to his fellow scholars.

Still, the receptionist at the newspaper recognized Norman, or at least his name, and made haste to summon Doyle Jeffries. Clad in a green eyeshade, vest, and shirtsleeves with garters holding them up, the editor ushered his caller back through a crowded space where machinery rumbled and vibrations shivered through the floor.

"The presses," Doyle said, raising his voice to make certain of being understood. "We print next door."

Norman had noticed the factory building attached to this one. "Is it time for a new edition already?"

"The advertising inserts you print ahead of time." Doyle waved his hand. "Here we are."

The editor's office proved to be a modest space partitioned to afford a measure of status and privacy. As he squeezed around behind the desk, Doyle said, "So, you decided to give me an interview after all?"

"Actually," Norman said, sitting down opposite the journalist, "I came to ask for help."

Doyle raised an eyebrow. "We reported the facts to the best of our ability. The way Sheriff Engle gave them to us and you supposedly gave them to him. If people think they don't add up, if they're looking at you funny, that's not the paper's fault."

Norman sighed. "I don't want you to run an editorial asserting my innocence or anything like that. This is something else. I need information. Facts about the history of Arkham."

As Doyle started to answer, someone screamed. Norman jerked in his chair and then realized the noise wasn't Schmidt—or any human being any human being at all. It was a train whistle sounding from the station to the south.

There was no chance Doyle had failed to notice his jumpiness, but the newspaperman did not see fit to remark on it. Instead, he said, "Well, in that case, let's make it tit for tat. You give me my interview, and afterward we can rummage through the morgue together."

Norman frowned in momentary perplexity, then realized the morgue in question was the newspaper's archives.

He did not want to be interviewed and repeat the falsehoods he and the sheriff had agreed upon, but he had come to Doyle recognizing that it might be necessary to secure the editor's cooperation. So he repeated the gist of his statement and answered questions as required.

They were shrewd, skeptical questions. Despite Doyle's genial manner, the inquisition made Norman feel as if his story were a balloon and each query a needle likely to pop it. He struggled against the impulse to try to make it more plausible via embellishment and over-explanation. He suspected such tactics might well result in non-sequiturs and inconsistencies.

Finally Doyle gave him a grin. "You hate lying, and you haven't had a lot of practice."

Norman tried to wrap himself in stiff scholarly dignity. "Naturally not."

"Even so, you're pretty good at it."

"I have no idea what you mean."

"Yeah, you do. Do you think you've delivered on your half of the bargain by peddling the same bunkum as before?"

"I think," Norman said, "that if you run an exclusive interview with the only witness to Professor Schmidt's disappearance, it won't matter if there's actually any new information in it. It will sell papers and keep interest in a sensational story alive a little longer."

Doyle laughed. "I'd almost think you'd been in the newspaper game yourself."

"No, but over the years, I've read enough of the popular press to notice how it goes about its business." Norman hesitated. "No offense."

"None taken, Professor. You've got us dead to rights. What information do you need?"

Norman removed Schmidt's list from his pocket, unfolded it, and handed it to the editor. "Whatever you can tell me about these places."

He had already decided he would be either revisiting the sites he had already seen, exploring ones he had not, or both. He had no other avenue of investigation. But before he did, he meant to learn everything he could about them. Although it seemed unlikely, there might be something that would shed light on how to reach Schmidt. Or at least, keep himself from suffering a similar fate.

Norman had started with the *Advertiser* on the supposition that a newspaper might record lurid stories or trivial oddities that more staid and scholarly sources would neglect. But if Doyle and his resources failed him, he would move on to the Arkham Historical Society and the stacks of the university's own Orne Library.

Doyle frowned at the paper. "This is Schmidt's list. The places you went together—including the farm—and the ones you hadn't gotten to yet."

Norman saw no hope of persuasively denying it. "He'd want his work to continue."

"This would be the same work you claimed not to understand? I think you're playing detective, Professor. Trying to find your friend. Does the sheriff have this list?"

"No." Sheriff Engle had not asked for it, nor had it occurred to Norman, still in shock from his ordeal, to offer the information.

"Great! Then it'll be just you and my photographer poking around like Sherlock Holmes and Dr. Watson."

For a moment, Norman felt a surge of excitement. It had never occurred to him that he might find a comrade to accompany him in his endeavors. To shore up his courage and share the danger—

But no. It was impossible. Without experiencing what he had, any such companion would think him demented, and even if it were otherwise, Norman could not ask someone else to face a peril that, for all he knew, was beyond any man's ability to withstand or even comprehend.

"I have to do my searching alone," he said, "but I promise you this. If I find Professor Schmidt, you'll be the first journalist to hear about it."

Doyle snorted. "And while the story you two are telling will probably just be more bunkum, at least it will be the *Advertiser's* exclusive bunkum?"

"Well…yes."

"I guess that will have to do." Doyle stood up. "Old editions are in the cellar, all the way back to when the *Advertiser* was the *Gazette*. Hope you don't mind a little dust."

Norman didn't, particularly, but the darkness and the shelving loaded with boxes reminded him of the dark barn and the stacks of whiskey crates. Dread knifed through him, and he paused on the creaking stairs.

Sensing his hesitation, Doyle glanced over his shoulder. "You all right?"

Norman took a breath. "Fine." He resumed his descent.

Over the years, someone had made an attempt to index the newspapers, but the results were sketchy at best. Still, this meager organization seemed to suffice for Doyle who, displaying an instinct for searching old documents that most academics would envy, unearthed the proper musty, yellowed newspapers with remarkable efficiency.

The accounts of the various locations described the disappearances that had captured Schmidt's interest, but, to Norman's surprise, they outlined other unfortunate occurrences as well. For example, in a house on Pickman Street, a young man and woman had hanged themselves on their wedding night. Off the highway that led to Newburyport, a superstitious mob had dragged a suspected witch from her cottage and kicked the poor old woman to death. A man living on Boundary Street had suffered from a phobia of bats and had gone to extraordinary lengths to trap and kill the animals, until the night a black cloud of them reportedly descended on him and ripped him to pieces. The stories suggested the sites on the list were unlucky, dangerous places, but Norman knew that already.

"Yeah," Doyle said, "I remember—" He sneezed. Apparently floating dust had tickled his nose.

"Remember what?" Norman asked.

"This fella. Jonathon Hobart Stane."

Norman frowned. "I've heard the name..."

"Well, you've lived in Arkham long enough that you would have." Doyle reached for a pocket handkerchief, remembered he was currently in vest and shirtsleeves, and settled for wiping his nose on his cuff. "But probably not for a while."

"Refresh my memory, please."

"A young man—well, young back when the paper was reporting on him and you were hearing about him—from one of those rich old families in French Hill that was hell-bent on giving away his inheritance. If you were collecting for a worthy cause, Stane was the soft touch you called on first."

Norman recalled seeing Stane's name on plaques around the university honoring donors for their contributions. He thought he might even have met Stane back in the days when he and Bernadine sometimes attended the college's social functions. But only a vague impression of a tall, good-looking young man escorting an equally attractive young lady remained.

"What happened in the Stane house?"

"In 1859, twin baby boys vanished from their cribs. The mother eventually threw herself out an upper-story window. In '81, a family member had a breakdown, spent some time locked up in the asylum, and lived out the rest of his days as a hopeless drunk. All in all, over the years, the Stanes picked up a reputation for being peculiar or at least unlucky. Although for a while, it seemed like Jonathon would turn that around. He had everything—money, looks, brains—and he was such a nice young man that nobody begrudged it to him." Doyle sighed. "Well, almost nobody."

"What do you mean?"

"After Congress declared war in '17, Jonathon was one of the first Arkham men to enlist. He and his fiancée were spending a last night together before he was due to report. Someone broke into the house, killed her with a big knife, like a Bowie, and probably left believing he'd killed Jonathon, too. But Jonathon held on until the surgeons at St. Mary's could patch him up. Later, he went to a private hospital in upstate New York for more operations. Obviously, he never made it to Europe."

"Did the police catch the culprit?"

"No," Doyle said. "It was an odd case. No forced entry, nothing stolen, no one with a motive. Just…savagery. The fact that no suspect was ever arrested may have helped to change Jonathon's temperament, not that it necessarily needed help after everything else he'd suffered."

"How did it change?"

"He came home from New York a recluse and something of a miser. So far as I know, he never gave another penny to charity. Not even to St. Mary's, where they saved his life."

"That's sad." Albeit understandable. Norman could imagine himself slipping into a similar misanthropy were he in Jonathon's place. "What finally became of him?"

"As far as I know," Doyle said, "he's still there, shut away in the mansion on Powder Mill Street. Nobody sees him anymore, though. He long ago fired the staff and has his groceries delivered."

"In that case," Norman said, "I know where to go next."

12

In Arkham, new money lived in Uptown, and a number of wealthy older families had moved there as well. With its imposing Huguenot, Georgian, and Colonial Revival houses, French Hill still proclaimed that in its day, *it* had been the city's fashionable, afflu-ent district. But many buildings were now in disrepair, in some cases manifestly derelict, with roofs half-denuded of shingles and lawns nearly as overgrown as the fields surrounding the barn where Schmidt had disappeared. A fair number of the yards were narrow enough that the old homes seemed to wall in the narrow cobbled streets. Or huddle together, as if conspiring.

As he climbed out of the Bearcat under a sky mountainous with thunderheads, Norman saw that the Stane family home, a two-story Georgian Colonial with a roof balustrade and three small gables protruding below, was not one of the dilapidated ones. Her-mit or not, the occupant must occasionally have someone cut the grass and possibly even slap on a new coat of paint. But every shut-ter was closed, which gave the astronomer the feeling that such cosmetic measures amounted to a mask intended to disguise a subtler form of decay.

With a scowl, he pushed trepidation away. He already knew the mansion, like the other sites on Schmidt's list, was unsafe. There was no use fretting over that. What mattered was that an ally might await him inside. He dropped the butt of his Chesterfield, crushed it under his brown Oxford, marched up to the door, and banged the knocker clasped in a brass lion's mouth.

No one answered. Perhaps, given that Jonathon Hobart Stane preferred solitude, Norman should have expected as much. He switched to knocking with his fist, then switched back when his knuckles started feeling tender. A housemaid came out onto the porch of a Victorian house across the street, peered at him, shook her head, and went back inside as though abandoning him to his folly.

"I didn't order anything," came a bass voice on the other side of the door, startling Norman even though it was exactly what he was trying to evoke with his repeated knocking.

"I'm not a delivery man," the scientist replied. "My name is Norman Withers. I'm an astronomy professor at Miskatonic, and I need to talk to you, Mr. Stane."

"Find another sucker. I don't give handouts anymore."

"So I've heard. But it's not about that, either. I know about cor-ners and the creatures that come out of them."

Stane hesitated a tick. "I don't know what you're talking about."

"I think you do. I think it was really one of the beasts that attacked you and your fiancée. You just couldn't say so for fear of being thought insane. I believe it because I survived such an encounter, too. Only I never actually saw one of the brutes. If you did, you have information I need."

"I don't care what you need."

"Please. It's urgent. So much so that I'm prepared to stand out here and knock all day if need be."

Stane barked a shrill, truncated little laugh. "You are, are you? Well, why not? The memories fester in a man's mind. It might do me good to lance the boil. Wait here."

Soft footsteps retreated and after a minute or so returned. The door swung open.

Stane was still a tall man, but above the waist, his body crooked to the left, presumably the result of his injuries. He wore slippers, pajamas, a silk dressing gown, and, over his head, a sack-like hood of dark red cloth. A blue eye gleamed behind the single hole on the right.

Norman offered his hand. Stane did not shake it.

"Come in if you're coming."

The interior of the house was every bit as gloomy as the closed shutters might have led one to expect. The air was close and stale, and every surface was dusty. Evidently Stane cared about keeping up appearances outside, but not within.

It was clear what he truly did care about. Strips of molding filled every space where wall met wall, floor, or ceiling, turning what would otherwise have been right angles into curves.

Similarly, every entry had a door, and each of those doors was shut, changing open rectangles into filled space. Stane opened one long enough to show his guest into a parlor sparsely furnished with Art Nouveau pieces made all of curves. The walls here, like those in the foyer, were devoid of picture frames.

"All of it, steps in the right direction," said Stane. Evidently he had noticed Norman taking in the details. "None of it sufficient. No one can eliminate every right or acute angle in a big old pile like this. Still, if I make it difficult enough for the creatures to find their way through, maybe I delay the inevitable. Sit."

Norman lowered himself onto one of the chairs. Insofar as he had ever thought about furniture at all, he liked the sturdy simple forms of William Morris and the Arts and Crafts Movement, but the somewhat flimsy-looking seat proved comfortable enough.

"It seems you've been rather hard at work trying to avoid another encounter with the beasts. What can you tell me about them?"

"You first," the hooded man replied.

Given that he was the one seeking assistance, Norman supposed that was fair. He told the story of Schmidt's disappearance and of his intent to rescue him.

At the end, Stane laughed. "You can't possibly believe the German's still alive."

"Can you be certain he isn't?"

Stane hesitated. "Well, not *absolutely* certain, I suppose. But the creatures are devils. The enemies of humanity in every sense."

"You say that because you've actually seen one?"

Stane laughed another sharp, short laugh. "Well, I have, and the slightest glimpse would be enough to convince a person of their maleficence, wouldn't it? To say nothing of watching the sweet, wonderful woman you love ripped apart by one of them and then feeling its claws tear into you. But I have more than firsthand experience to draw on. I've made a study of them."

"How?" Norman asked. "They aren't merely a species unknown to science. They normally exist in a place or a condition science can't even observe."

"You only think that because you don't realize the ancients knew truths modern scientists have yet to rediscover. Einstein, and his disciples like your friend Schmidt, are just starting to walk the paths others trod before them." Stane yipped his hyena laugh. "And now you know where those paths lead."

Norman sighed. "It sounds like you're talking about mysticism."

"And you sound like you've just decided I can't possibly have anything worthwhile to tell you. Open your mind, Professor. Rutherford proved the things we perceive as solid are mere ghosts, empty space with a haze of tiny particles suspended in the void. Hubble demonstrated the universe is vast beyond comprehension, with the Milky Way only one of countless galaxies. Einstein taught us time and space are one, and malleable to boot. In each case, the ancients—well, a few of the ancients—were there before them. More to the point, they recorded their observations of the particular phenomena that now concern you."

It was the final comment that gave Norman pause. Although he remained skeptical that Stane's "ancients" truly had anything to teach the twentieth century about theoretical physics or astronomy, it was not beyond the realm of possibility that some philosopher had observed something about the creatures or the opening and closing of breaches that might prove of practical use. In any case, if he needed to listen to a load of mumbo jumbo to hear what Stane himself had experienced, so be it.

"Please excuse me," Norman said. "I'm eager to learn whatever you can tell me. If my manner seemed to indicate otherwise, it's because this is all very new and strange."

Stane laughed. "You have no idea how strange. The creatures that took your friend are Hounds of Tindalos."

"Hounds?"

"Sometimes they hunt in packs like hounds. They howl like hounds. But of course they aren't really. We don't have a word for what they are. We probably aren't even capable of seeing them as they truly are. So 'Hounds' is as good a name as any."

"And 'Tindalos'?"

"That might be the name—" Stane turned his head from side to side. He seemed to be listening. Stiff with alarm, Norman did the same but heard nothing.

The hooded man relaxed. "Sorry. I jump at shadows sometimes. As I was saying, Tindalos might be the name of the place they come from. Or the god they serve. Or maybe the place and the god are somehow one and the same."

Norman grunted. "Your ancients don't appear to have been certain of much."

"Naturally not. How easy do you think it was to study something that spends most of its time removed from the world as we experience it and kills whomever's around when it does come through? Still, they discovered a few facts and built some interesting hypotheses around them. They conjectured that the Hounds' home is so far in the past that time itself takes on a different aspect. In our age, it's curved, just as Einstein proclaims. In theirs, it's angular."

Norman frowned. "I'm not sure what that would mean."

"Nor am I. Nor, quite possibly, were they. But let's suppose they were right. Your hero Einstein tells us time and space are ultimately the same thing. Then maybe right and acute angles provide trails and doorways for the Hounds to reach us here in our reality."

Norman mulled that over. "If everything you're suggesting is true, and if Schmidt's ideas are also true, a disproportionate number of those trails lead to Arkham. Do you have any idea why that would be?"

"I can only guess. Perhaps once a Hound opens a 'breach,' as you call them, its pack mates can sense the path and the doorway. That makes it somewhat more likely that a second creature will eventually push through somewhere nearby. And if your luck is running bad enough that you get to the point where there's a whole spider web of entry points..." Stane shrugged his crooked shoulders.

Norman realized that, despite himself, he was starting to take these notions seriously. Perhaps, when one encountered a phenomenon utterly beyond the realm of normal human experience, one grasped at any explanation, no matter how dubious the source.

"But why do they come here?" he asked. "Can't they catch prey in their own time?"

"Perhaps not the right sort of prey." Once again, Stane stopped abruptly, then sniffed with sufficient force to indent the fabric of his hood. Norman took a wary sniff of his own without detecting any trace of the putrid vapor from the barn.

"One source claims," Stane continued, "that we humans have something special inside us that the Hounds either hunger for or lust to destroy, and so they kill us to get at it."

"And Schmidt attracted their attention by repeatedly poking around at the discontinuity points."

"Possibly. It seems like it."

Norman pondered his next question. So much remained unknown, so much that he needed to understand, that it was difficult to pursue an organized line of inquiry.

"When the bootlegger fired his pistol," he said, "it seemed to stop the Hound that was stalking him, at least momentarily. I hope that means they can be hurt."

Stane laughed. "I haven't discouraged you yet? Heaven knows, I'm trying. I think they can be *startled*. Disconcerted by fleeting twinges of pain. I doubt they can truly be crippled or killed."

"What's your basis for thinking that?"

"The pistol didn't save the bootlegger, did it? And on the night I was attacked, I'd hauled out my father's old revolver and cavalry saber from his Rough Rider days. I suppose I thought looking at them would put me in a military state of mind for the AEF." Stane laughed.

"When the Hound lunged out of the shadows and pounced on Barbara," the crooked man continued, "I grabbed the sword. By the time I turned back around, the creature was springing at me. It bore me down and savaged me, and I stabbed it as best I could. Eventually it broke off and disappeared."

"Isn't that reason to think you *did* hurt it?"

"I don't think so. It retreated too quickly. Too nimbly. It seems more likely that it had fed well enough to satisfy it and had grown tired of the repeated pinpricks."

"Well, making the creatures slow down and with luck even turn away is better than nothing, I suppose. Now tell me this. How do they open and close the holes, and is there a way for a human being to do the same?"

"They don't need to 'open and close' anything. For them, corners are always passages into our time and place. They simply have to find their way to them."

Norman waited for more. When Stane failed to offer anything further, he said, "You didn't answer the second half of my question."

"You can't *still* be thinking of trying to rescue Professor Schmidt. The man is dead!"

"You conceded we don't know that."

"Even if he were alive, you couldn't do anything for him. You'd only throw away your own life and risk stirring up the Hounds. Imagine the slaughter if they started hunting in Arkham every day instead of once every several years."

That was a ghastly thought, but Norman hoped it was also pure speculation. "The fact that you're working so hard to dissuade me makes me think there must be a way for people to go through."

"Well, there isn't. So go home and forget all this."

"If I can't open a discontinuity myself, the other option is to station myself at a breach point and wait for a Hound to notice me. Perhaps if I'm prepared..." Norman realized Stane was no longer paying attention.

Rather, the hooded man was jumping up from his seat and casting about more wildly than before. "They're here!" he screamed. "They're here!"

Norman looked around just as frantically. He saw, heard, smelled, and felt nothing that would lead him to believe the Hounds were coming.

Taking a ragged breath, his heartbeat slowing, he decided that even if some of Stane's information was accurate, the poor man's ordeal had left him with a nervous disorder from which he had never recovered. Perhaps a well-wisher could calm him down, at least temporarily. He turned to try, then froze when he saw the little revolver in the hooded man's hand. It was pointed at his torso.

Stane must have taken advantage of Norman's distraction to whisk the weapon from the pocket of his dressing gown or from under a cushion. Now he laughed and laughed at what was no doubt the stupefaction on the older man's face.

━━ 13 ━━

"There's no reason for this," Norman said, his voice tremulous. "I'm not your enemy."

"Maybe not on purpose," Stane replied, "but it's clear you aren't going to leave this matter alone, and I really don't want a fool stirring things up. Who knows where it would lead?" He shifted the barrel of the revolver to indicate the door that opened on the foyer, then shifted it back. "Out, then right, then down the hall to the left."

As he approached the door, Norman wondered if he could lunge through, slam it behind him, and dash outside the house, all so quickly the hooded man wouldn't be able to shoot him in the back. To say the least, it seemed improbable, and the moment passed without him finding the boldness to make the attempt.

Instead, he said, "People know I'm here. My car is parked right outside."

"That complicates things," Stane replied, "but it's not all that difficult. I can call a man who'll drive your car away, no questions asked. And the police aren't likely to pry into the affairs of a wealthy invalid all that aggressively. Should worst come to worst, I have a firm of excellent attorneys on retainer."

"Look," Norman said, "I see now that I was on the verge of making a terrible mistake. If there's nothing a human being can do against the Hounds, then of course I should leave them alone. Just let me go, and I swear I won't say anything about this…" He groped for an inoffensive word, a word that wouldn't incite a lunatic to instant violence. "Misunderstanding."

Stane laughed. "Nice try, Professor. Truly. But I'm afraid there's another side to it, too."

"What other side?"

"I'll tell you once you're through that door straight ahead."

The door in question looked like it belonged in a prison or asylum for the criminally insane, not in a mansion like this. An oversize steel deadbolt latch held it shut, and a round, barred window not much bigger than a fist provided a glimpse of the darkness waiting on the other side.

Norman opened the door. He didn't realize Stane had stepped up close behind him until the hooded man shoved him through. Norman stumbled, nearly fell, and the door slammed behind him. The latch clanged as Stane twisted it down to secure it to the strike plate.

A moment later, the light in the ceiling came on, revealing an unfurnished room with a bricked-up window. Unlike every other portion of the house Norman had seen, this room had right-angle corners unaltered by molding. Painted in dark blue and ocher pigment, geometrical designs adorned the walls with some sort of glyphs written around them.

Norman pivoted back toward the door. Stane was peering through the peephole with his good—or was it his only?—eye. Norman felt a sudden furious and quite uncharacteristic impulse to try to gouge the eye through the bars.

But even in the unlikely event that he could accomplish such a feat, it wouldn't help him. He took a ragged breath and said, "All right. Now tell me."

Stane laughed. "Back in the parlor, I didn't get around to explaining *everything* I've gleaned about the Hounds. It hasn't been easy, but the hints are there in the *Livre d'Eibon*, the *Pnakotic Manuscripts,* and even comparatively modern sources like Prinn and d'Erlette if a person knows how to interpret them. One thing I picked up and rather to my dismay—" The crooked man interrupted himself with another shrill titter of mirth. "On those rare occasions when a man escapes the Hounds, he doesn't always *stay* escaped. Sooner or later, they're apt to come after him."

On another occasion, that revelation would have chilled Norman, but now he had more immediate problems. "Don't you see? That's all the more reason for you to work with me to find ways to thwart them."

"You'd think so, wouldn't you? But I already have a strategy. Appease them. Feed a dog, and it's less likely to take a bite out of you. Or in my case, *another* bite." Stane giggled.

"You're sacrificing people."

"If you care to think of it that way. It's easier than you'd imagine. Some theatrical makeup combined with the bad light outdoors at night and I don't look too horribly ugly. And the people I approach on one pretext or another—hobos, drunks, whores, Ethels—aren't picky. I collect them out of town, and a nip from a drugged flask keeps them docile until I get them home."

"It's monstrous! How can you live with yourself?"

"Ever since that night, I've seen life differently. I *remember* loving Barbara, but I've never cared that the creature tore her apart. Better her than me. I don't care when a Hound kills one of my offerings, either. To tell the truth, I like to watch."

"So you intend to hold me prisoner until a Hound shows up?"

"Ah, that would be grounds for hope, now wouldn't it? Under normal circumstances, it could be weeks, months, or even years before a Hound manifests in this particular space. Plenty of time for someone to come looking for you. But I'm not leaving the entity's arrival to chance. 'Mysticism' affords me the means of lighting a beacon to draw it here. It's actually rather easy for someone in my psychically aberrant condition."

With that, Stane took a step back from the door and began to recite. The sounds had sufficient differentiation and cadence to suggest actual words and sentences, but they weren't in any language Norman had ever encountered. The shrill, staccato yips and snarls were more reminiscent of a hyena than the madman's laughter.

Lightheaded and short of breath, Norman told himself that, despite all the uncanny events he'd experienced hitherto, arrant witchcraft was a step too far. Clearly, Stane was delusional, and nothing would happen in response to an incantation.

Then a pulse of blue and ocher light illuminated the door and the wall around it. Norman turned. The painted designs and symbols were glowing, brightening and fading in a rhythm like a heartbeat. They looked three-dimensional as well, but inconsistently so. One moment, they stood out from the walls, the next, they seemed farther away, like lamps shining through mist.

Stane brayed laughter at his prisoner's consternation. Norman's light-headedness whirled into outright vertigo, and his stomach churned with nausea.

He scrambled to one of the geometric figures, a tangle of octagons pierced by isosceles triangles. It flattened back into two dimensions when he came within reach of it, and he clawed it with his fingernails. Chips of paint flaked away from the plaster beneath.

"Good thought!" called Stane. "But you can't possibly do enough damage in the time you have left."

The assurance in the hooded man's voice made Norman believe him. But what else was there to do except attempt to deface the paintings? He cast about for an alternative and found nothing. The cell was empty, the window sealed, the sturdy door secured from the other side—

Or was it? The door hung on three barrel hinges. When it was closed as it was currently, the screws that held the hinges to the frame and door were inaccessible, but the pivots and cylinders were on his side of the barrier.

He emptied his pockets. They proved to contain his wallet and paper money, his keys, a Mercury dime, two buffalo nickels, a pencil stub, a crumpled pack of Chesterfields, and a matchbook with two matches left. Why wasn't he carrying his Barlow knife?

Too late to worry about it now. He'd have to work with the makeshift tools at his disposal. He scurried to the door and inspected the hinges.

The pivots had screw caps on top to anchor them in the cylinders.

Experimenting, he found that the dime just barely fit the notch in the uppermost. He gripped the coin between thumb and forefinger and attempted to twist the cap counterclockwise. It resisted.

As he strained, a familiar sense of malevolent scrutiny stabbed through him, and he gasped. Evidently sensing it, too, Stane giggled.

But the Hound didn't burst from whatever corner it occupied. Not yet. Perhaps, for all its ferocity, it possessed a measure of caution as well.

"What are you doing?" asked Stane. The small window didn't afford a view of a person at the edge of the door.

Norman didn't answer. He was too busy struggling with the screw. Finally, grudgingly, it yielded a hair, balked once more, and then rotated all the way out.

With it removed, he slid the pin out the bottom of the cylinder. He stuck it in his hip pocket and went to work on the middle one.

Unfortunately, the second cap was screwed down even tighter, and the groove seemed narrower and shallower, or perhaps fear was making Norman's fingers clumsier. In any case, the dime skipped repeatedly out of the notch while the fastener refused to yield.

The sense of being watched intensified. Surely the Hound would soon emerge into the sacrificial chamber.

That meant Norman had no hope of removing all three pivots in time if, in fact, it was possible at all. Terrified, frustrated, he slammed the heel of his hand against the door. With the top pin extracted, it shook a little in its frame.

"What are you doing?" Stane repeated, only now in a different tone. Gloating cruelty had given way to alarm.

Norman realized that while *he* knew he wasn't going to get all three hinges disassembled, his captor didn't. Was it conceivable that he could "double shuffle" Stane into doing something foolish?

Not if he sounded desperate. Swallowing, he resolved to imitate the cool, superior confidence with which Sherlock Holmes, A. J. Raffles, and Boston Blackie spoke to their adversaries. He'd read their exploits in his younger days, before he decided he had no time for such diversions anymore.

"I'm taking down the door," he said. "I'll have it open in a few moments." He gave it another thump.

"That's impossible," Stane replied.

"Did you hang it yourself? I suppose I shouldn't be surprised you did such a flimsy job of it. Rich boys don't have much experience with manual labor, do they?"

"You're wasting your time. The deadbolt will hold up the door."

"All by itself? Don't be ridiculous. And with the way open, I wonder whom the Hound will attack: A stranger? Or the man it mauled years ago and has been sniffing around for ever since? You told me they like to finish what they start." Norman pulled the pivot from his pocket and dropped it to clink on the floor. "That's two pins out."

Metal scraped as the barrel of Stane's revolver slid through the bars at an angle. Norman cringed, but when the gun flashed and banged, the shots missed. The window was too small and the bars too close together for the firearm to swivel far enough to the side to hit a target in his current position.

"Nice try," Norman said, dropping to one knee. Stane couldn't see him, but he might be able to tell from what height his voice was coming. "I'm going after the last pin. Here it comes." He gave the door another thump.

A putrid-smelling gray vapor, so thin it was difficult to see in the inadequate light of the ceiling fixture, washed over him. The Hound was surely coming any second now.

Stane seemingly caught the stench as well, and it spurred him to further action. "Damn you!" he screamed. The deadbolt latch clanked as he disengaged it to enter the cell and eliminate the supposed threat to the integrity of the door.

Norman stood up. When the door swung open, he waited an instant, then shoved it as hard as he could.

The door caught Stane halfway in, halfway out, and slammed him into the frame. Norman pulled the heavy door back and pounded it into the hooded man again. Then, praying he'd stunned his captor, he scrambled around the door. At his back, the Hound howled.

Stane wasn't stunned, at least not sufficiently so to keep him from aiming the revolver at Norman. A shock ran through the floor as the Hound made a first bound forward.

Norman flailed and, more by luck than any pugilistic skill, swatted the firearm out of line. He grabbed hold of Stane's robe and swung him out of the doorway and into the cell.

In the process, he caught a glimpse of a rearing serpentine shape with crocodilian jaws and a long tongue lashing beyond. But Stane's reeling, floundering body partially blocked the view, and for that he was grateful. He suspected that, had he seen it any more clearly, he might have frozen despite the urgency of the moment.

He fled through the space he'd cleared, yanked the door shut behind him, and secured the deadbolt latch. An instant later, an impact jolted the barrier so violently that, even though he'd really only removed one pin, he feared it actually would fall down. Trembling, he backed away.

More thuds followed. So did a snapping sound that was presumably gnashing jaws. So did Stane's screams.

The crooked man's face abruptly appeared behind the window. The hood was gone, revealing a left profile ridged and grooved with scar tissue and an empty eye socket in the midst of the ruined flesh. "Help me!" he wailed.

Despite what he now knew about Stane's murders, despite what the man had tried to do to him personally, at that moment, Norman *wanted* to help. But it was impossible. Even if he could muster the courage to reopen the door, doing so would only be throwing his own life away.

Neither hand nor paw but something in between, smeared with a bluish grease or slime and terminating in a bristling bundle of hooked claws, reached over Stane's head. It snagged the talons under its victim's mouth and pulled upward, tearing his face away and obliterating his remaining eye as it ripped its way along. Then the beast yanked Stane down and out of sight.

The thudding and screaming lasted a few more seconds. Then came a sucking or slurping sound. Then silence, at which point the vile-smelling vapor drifting through the round little window began to dissipate.

Ready to turn tail at the slightest new sound, the merest hint of renewed activity on the other side of the door, Norman crept forward. His judgment told him the danger was probably past. His raw nerves, however, screamed that the Hound was still there, that it was just waiting for him to come closer. Then it would find a way to seize him, the barrier notwithstanding.

He peered through the bars and could see nothing but walls,

floor, ceiling, the sealed window, and the designs and sigils. The glow that had shined from the latter had all but faded away.

Unfortunately, Norman could not see the entire cell any more than Stane had been able to. He gave the door a thump from this side thinking that might provoke the Hound into revealing itself if it was still present. There was no reaction.

Probably he should let it go at that, but his very dread impelled him to make absolutely certain the creature had departed. He took a breath, slid back the deadbolt latch, and eased open the door, ready to yank it closed again at any sign of danger.

The Hound was gone. As was Stane, and, as far as Norman could see, every drop of spilled blood. Only the madman's hood remained, the scarlet cloth now smeared with bluish sludge. Two more streaks of the same jelly lead to the far left corner.

—— 14 ——

Norman prowled through the shadowy, sparsely furnished house with its molding softening every corner and its shutters holding in its secrets. The air was as stale and dusty as before. Now that the Hound had taken its prey and gone, the only sounds were the soft ticking of a clock somewhere and the creak of floorboards under his feet.

He did not *want* to linger here but had resolved to stay in order to search for the documents Stane had mentioned. He had learned a good deal since his arrival—albeit, none of it encouraging—but he still did not know how to reach Tindalos, if that was really the name for the realm of the Hounds. Although the crooked man had claimed otherwise, perhaps his research held the answer.

To Norman's disappointment, the library on the first floor contained only mundane material, volumes by Twain, Melville, Hawthorne, and Scott, business ledgers, and the 1911 edition of the *Encyclopedia Britannica*. But when he explored the upper reaches of the mansion, he found that Stane had transformed one of the three small gabled rooms into a more idiosyncratic place for study.

More painted sigils and hieroglyphs adorned the walls, and grotesque little carvings, one a jade figurine of a seated figure with a betentacled head, reposed on the curved shelving along with an assortment of books. To Norman's surprise, some were the works of men like Plato, Aristotle, Bentham, and Kant along with commentaries hereon. Books on philosophy, with an emphasis on ethics. They pointed to a time when Jonathon Hobart Stane had pondered the question of how to live a moral life, and the depraved murderer he had become had evidently believed the musings of conventional philosophers had at least a little bearing on the esoteric matters that preoccupied him later on.

Norman closed the door. He did not want any open rectangular spaces, either, not in this house. Then, guided by Stane's references to the ancients, he scanned the shelves for especially old-looking books.

There was only one, bound in cracked and crumbling blue leather. Apparently Stane had somehow managed to consult other tomes without acquiring them for his personal collection.

Careful not to damage the book more than time had already, Norman opened it. Faded and difficult to make out against the brittle and blotchy-brown title page, woodblock printing in blue ink proclaimed this was the *Livre d'Eibon*.

Norman started looking through it and discovered a consistent patter of two printed pages followed by two blanks. For all he knew, that had some arcane significance, but he suspected it was an artifact of the archaic production process.

The book also interspersed blocks of text with diagrams and glyphs like the ones in the cell and on the walls of this room, evidence, if more were needed, that it truly did contain information concerning the Hounds.

Near the end was a different sort of drawing. Dots radiating lines—representing stars, perhaps?—hung in a void, and a clawed, six-fingered hand reached as though to pick them like berries or perhaps simply crush them from existence.

Norman stared at the page in stupefaction. He had determined that, bizarre as it seemed, Stane's ancients truly had comprehended space-time, and the entities that prowled its hidden pathways like game trails in a jungle, in a way modern scientists did not. Was it possible they had also known something about the heavens that shed light on his own astronomical conundrum?

With an effort of will, he forced himself to stop staring. The crude picture could mean anything, and there would be time enough to investigate it further if he survived his present course of action. For now, his priority was using what he had found to go after Schmidt.

Assuming he could. The text appeared to be in French, possibly medieval French. Whatever it was, Norman could not read it.

Perhaps he could prevail on one of his colleagues at Miskatonic—maybe Professor Rice from Classical Languages—to translate. But he would not be able to convince the man that time was of the essence. He would only sound crazy if he tried.

A half-dozen identical, slim, black-bound journals sat on the shelf between the spot the *Livre d'Eibon* had occupied and a soapstone carving of a man in a pharaoh's headdress with an expression of sly mockery on his face. Norman opened the first of the books, beheld the initial words handwritten therein, and exclaimed in satisfaction.

Stane had taken notes as he made his studies—notes in English. Norman flipped through the volumes in turn.

It appeared that, as he had more or less indicated to Norman, the madman had consulted four books of esoteric wisdom: the *Livre d'Eibon*; the *Pnakotic Manuscripts*; *Cultes des Goules* by Francois-Honore Balfour, Comte d'Erlette; and *De Vermiis Mysteriis* by Ludwig Prinn. From each, Stane had gleaned something of the nature of the Hounds of Tindalos. Some of it, he had already relayed to Norman. Other bits were new, including the revelation that the creatures possessed allies: the "Dholes"—whatever they were—and satyrs.

Could the latter possibly be correct? Norman imagined the goat men from classical mythology, as depicted in ancient paintings and sculptures, and decided it was unlikely the Hounds made common cause with anything that close to being human. The term as employed here almost certainly applied to entities more alien and malign.

After a second, he surprised himself by laughing. It may have been an inappropriate response, possibly even a warning sign of an impending breakdown, but he was already in so far over his head that, at this moment, the discovery that he might have to contend with other monsters in addition to the Hounds seemed more comical than alarming.

He continued skimming. In the fifth volume was the incantation for "lighting the beacon" to call the Hounds. And in the sixth, another spell, likewise rendered phonetically, for "splitting the angle" and walking through time in the flesh.

Of course, the spell could be nonsense. Norman's understanding of science insisted it had to be. But after what he had experienced in the cell, he could only believe that somehow, in some fashion, magical conjurations sometimes did what they were alleged to, and in all likelihood this was one of them.

If so, he supposed he should be glad that, against all odds, he had accomplished a crucial step on the way to his ultimate goal. Yet he felt cold with the knowledge that now it was actually possible to follow through on his resolve.

Part Three

Tindalos

═══ 15 ═══

Norman had never frequented Arkham's speakeasies—or "juice joints," to use Schmidt's parlance—but other faculty and students at Miskatonic had a propensity for doing so. Over time, as if by osmosis, Norman had absorbed a little information about them. Supposedly there were a couple with some pretensions to "class." The Nightingale Club in Uptown was one, and the Tick Tock Club in the Merchant District was another.

Located outside the city limits on the highway to Boston, Hibb's Roadhouse affected no such airs. Sawdust covered the floor, the walls were made of bare planks, and the place shook when a train clattered past on the tracks nearby. The air stank of beer and the sweat of the factory workers and farmers who had crowded in to do their drinking. Some of those regulars eyed Norman curiously as he made his way through the press.

He wondered why, as a phone call to Doyle Jeffries had revealed, Old Sadie Sheldon frequented Hibb's and not some fancier establishment. Maybe the bootlegger was a silent partner in the roadhouse. Or perhaps roosting here was a way of proclaiming that, born and raised on a little farm outside Dunwich, he still retained the common touch.

If it was the latter, Sheldon was only willing to put up with so much to foster that image. Despite the general crush, the bootlegger and five associates had the back of the room to themselves with the adjacent tables vacant. A big man in a sack suit intercepted Norman as he approached.

"You can drink at the bar," the hoodlum said. He waved his hand in that direction.

"Thank you," Norman replied, "but I came to speak with Mr. Sheldon."

Eyes narrowing, the big man looked him over a second time. Norman got the distinct impression that people with a scholarly air about them did not seek out Old Sadie Sheldon very often. "And who are you?"

"Norman Withers. The person who told the police about the barn full of whiskey outside of town."

"Damn," the hoodlum said. "Wait here." He went to the table, talked back and forth with his boss for a moment, and then waved Norman forward.

Old Sadie Sheldon was a small man with a high forehead over dark, deep-set eyes in nests of wrinkles. He still projected a gamecock toughness despite his advancing years. He wore his steel-gray thinning hair brushed straight back and slicked down with brilliantine.

Like his subordinate, he took his time looking Norman over. At length he said, "After people interfere in my business, they mostly go out of their way to avoid me."

Norman put his hand on the back of an empty chair. "May I sit?"

Sheldon snorted. "Sure, why not?"

Norman took a seat while Sheldon continued to grin silently.

"Like I was saying, normally, if you'd found the brown and run to the cops, I'd be annoyed. Hell, maybe I am. I haven't decided yet. But I understand there was more to it. You had a friend go missing. One of my boys went missing too, same place, same night, although from what I understand, you and the German never saw him."

"That's what my statement said," Norman answered, "but it's not true. Professor Schmidt and I did run into him."

The gangsters at the table tensed. "Then tell us what happened to him."

Norman sighed. "You wouldn't believe it so it would only get in our way. Suffice it to say, I regret that your associate is probably dead. *Not* by Professor Schmidt's hand or mine, I assure you. But if he's alive and I can restore him to you, I will."

"What is this shit?" Sheldon snarled. "What are you beating your gums about?"

"I know it's frustrating. This is difficult to discuss, and I'm handling it awkwardly. I apologize."

"To hell with *you apologize!* Do you think that because we're meeting in a public place, you can play games with me? I can come pay you a visit anytime I want!"

Norman waved his hand. "Obviously. But there's no reason it should come to that if we conduct ourselves like reasonable men."

Sheldon glared for another moment, and then his gaze softened. "You're not even a little bit afraid of me, are you?" he asked.

With a twinge of surprise, Norman realized it was so.

He had no illusions that he had transformed into a courageous man. The terror he had felt in the presence of the Hounds and the recurring stabs of dread that afflicted him afterward sufficed to disabuse him of any such notion. Yet his recent experiences had transposed fear up an octave into the register of the otherworldly. Ordinary human beings, even hardened criminals, were no longer striking the proper notes.

"I'm not," he said. "Sorry."

Sheldon laughed. "What *are* you doing here if not to tell me what happened to Frankie—my fella standing guard?"

"I need some things. Perhaps I could buy them myself, but not without people who already have their suspicions about me wondering why. I imagine a man in your position could obtain them discreetly." He extracted a piece of notepaper from his breast pocket and handed it over.

Sheldon's eyes widened as he read the list. "Hell, Professor, haven't you heard? The war's over. They signed the Armistice back in '18."

"I still need them, I'll never tell anyone where I got them. And, of course, I expect to pay for them." Norman removed an envelope from his jacket's inner pocket and handed it across the table.

Sheldon riffled through the bills. "Teaching college must pay pretty good."

"After my wife—my ex-wife—remarried, I didn't owe alimony anymore, and I worked such long hours that I didn't have the chance to spend much money. My pay just accumulated in the bank. It's all yours if you help me."

Frowning, his eyes narrowed, Sheldon pondered through three sips of whiskey. Then he said, "I probably shouldn't. But scratch is scratch, and I'm curious to see if you'll show up in the *Advertiser* doing something crazy."

"With luck, the *Advertiser* will never find out about it. I do have one condition before we make a deal."

"Oh, yeah? What's that?"

"Someone will need to show me how to use the items." Norman smiled. "I am just a college teacher, after all."

16

The Prohibition Agents had smashed all the whiskey crates and the bottles within, filling the old barn with the lingering smell of whiskey. After that, they had had no reason to remain. No one challenged Norman when he entered, set his fused bundle of dynamite in the corner where Schmidt had vanished, and then stood facing the juncture of the two walls with Stane's copied incantation in hand. He assumed that if any pathway would take him to the physicist, it was the one that ran from here.

He felt ridiculous with the M1921 Thompson submachine gun and its ammunition, like a little boy playing soldier. Or an aging pack mule weighted down with too much baggage. Yet in a way, the absurdity was welcome. It provided a distraction from the fear.

He had twice survived the Hounds' attentions by running away. It was surreal that he, a mild-mannered academic his whole life through, now proposed to venture *toward* them. Indeed, to invade their home territory.

Certainly, he had little faith that his new weapon would actually enable him to survive. Stane had said it likely would not. Still, if it could improve his chances even marginally, it was worth having.

Of course, that was assuming the Hounds even got the chance to accost him. For all he knew, he was about to step into a place without oxygen, or where blazing heat or unbearable cold would destroy him in an instant. Stane's notes claimed that the same incantation that opened the way protected a traveler from adverse conditions, but Norman wondered how far he could trust that given that the madman had surely never made the journey himself. Stane had done his homicidal best to stay clear of the Hounds except under the safest conditions he could devise.

All in all, Norman would be taking a colossal risk when it did seem all but certain Schmidt was dead. Yet despite all the factors that might have deterred a wiser man, he realized he was going through with it.

He owed it to Schmidt to attempt a rescue so long as there was even the slimmest hope, and the scientist in him wanted to see what lay beyond the human world, even if that meant plunging into horror. To deny those instincts would diminish him, possibly shrivel him back into something he no longer cared to be.

Or maybe it was simply that decisions and events generated momentum, and now that he had come this far, turning back would be the greatest absurdity of all. Whatever his motives, he supposed he should stop pondering them and get on with the task at hand before his nerve failed him.

Norman started reading from the paper. He had rehearsed by practicing this a sentence at a time, out of sequence, to minimize the chances of botching the recitation or casting the spell prematurely. Stane's notes suggested that could be dangerous, although he was vague about the specific consequences.

The yipping, rasping words strained his throat, but as best he could judge, they came out properly, and as he declaimed the final sentence, the world changed. Although the corner he was facing looked no different, it *felt* not just open but profoundly so. As if a door had swung open on a vast desert or a gulf as deep and broad as the Grand Canyon.

The sensation made the hairs on the back of his neck stand on end, but at least he did not feel the attention of a Hound lurking beyond the threshold. He took a breath, walked gingerly forward, and this time penetrated the point where two walls came together with a light sensation like the strands of a bead curtain brushing over his body.

· · ·

17

Beyond the corner, twilight waited. Taking a first look around, Norman found himself on a white path that zigzagged forward over gray emptiness without any form of visible support. The way was ten feet wide and broad enough that someone who kept to the center need not fear falling over the side. Even so, the drop-off into what appeared to be infinite depths made him feel dizzy and sick.

He took a breath and then a small experimental step that felt no different than walking on a sidewalk. Turning, he discovered that he stood on the end of the path and that the very end was shaped like a right-angle notch. He reached beyond it and felt the bead-curtain sensation on his fingers. They disappeared, presumably back into the barn, and reappeared when he retracted his arm.

So everything was all right so far. Either because somehow there was naturally air here, or through the intercession of the spell he had cast, he could breathe. The temperature was cool but not cold. There was light to see by. Gravity and friction made ambulation possible even though he could discern no planetary body beneath him. The path looked smooth as glass, and the way back to the human world was open.

All in all, conditions were as favorable as he had any right to expect. Still, he needed three more deep steadying breaths before he could impel himself farther down the path.

As he neared the first jag, the vast space around him stirred and seethed. Sure the Hounds or their allies were converging on him, he let out a choked little cry.

But no creatures had noticed the intruder and roused themselves to destroy him. Not yet. Rather, by advancing deeper into the void, Norman had somehow brought his environs into clearer focus. His was only one of countless paths, the others suspended above, below, and to either side of him, receding until they faded into the gloom. Some were angular, and some curved. Here and there, one met another. Where they ran on the same level, they crossed via a simple intersection. Where they existed at differing elevations, ramps slanted and spirals coiled.

Once he recovered from the misapprehension that the Hounds had discovered him, Norman still found the spectacle before him, if not terrifying, at least disconcerting. A moment ago, it had appeared he was on a road that, however dangerous, ran straight to his destination. Now it seemed he needed to pick his way through a labyrinth.

As if in response to his dismay, a hitherto unsuspected faculty, surely another product of Stane's magic, opened inside him. He *felt* he was heading in the right direction. In the same way, perhaps, that a flower sensed the sun. When he thought of the barn, the sensation flipped to point back the way he had come.

The faculty guided him through two choice points. Then, sharpening into something akin to clairvoyance, it began providing glimpses of what lay at the ends of the paths he was passing by.

One led to a darkened dormitory in what might have been a Dickensian workhouse, where gaunt, pale women slept motionless as corpses in their cots. Another to a room with paper walls where an Asian man was cutting open his own abdomen with a short sword. A third, to a sidewalk where a mother and child stared up at some sort of airship about to crash into one of two prodigious towers.

If all was going as intended, Norman's route was taking him from the present into a past remote beyond imagining, but the branching trails led to sites and moments in both the past and future, essentially randomly. The one constant was that the termini were rooms, streets, constructed places, because, far more than Nature, they provided the clearly defined angles required for breaches. It was strange to reflect that if humans had never invented their arts and sciences, they would have lived lives that were, to borrow Hobbes's phrase, "nasty, brutish, and short," but they might largely have avoided the predations of the Hounds.

The next side trail zigzagged through emptiness to a room where several brown, beetle-like creatures, each standing on its hind legs and with tools hanging in metal loops riveted to their carapaces, were working to construct or repair some type of machine. As one, they turned in Norman's direction. Their split black eyes stared, and their antennae quivered.

Dear Lord, could they sense him in the same manner he'd sensed the scrutiny of the Hounds? He hurried onward.

No beetle-thing entered the maze to pursue him, but the incident nonetheless served to remind him he was in danger with every step he took. He needed to stop sightseeing down the intersecting paths and stay focused and vigilant.

He adhered to that resolve and several minutes later—if "minutes" was a word that meant anything here—approached an intersection different than any he had traversed hitherto. Before him, his zigzagging path crossed a curved trail coiling up from below. At the spot where they met, a red circle eclipsed the whiteness of the walkways.

As far as Norman knew, there was no inherent reason why a point where angular and curved time intersected should pose a problem, but on the other hand, any new feature of the maze could prove hazardous. He prowled forward even more warily than before.

Nothing appeared to threaten him. He sighed, slumped, and in that moment of relative relaxation, something gleamed at the periphery of his vision. Reflexively, he turned toward the light.

At the end of the curved trail, a Stutz Bearcat sped down a highway between wooded green hills on a sunlit day. Norman's vantage point put him in the car, perched behind the two seats and affording him a close-up view of himself and Bernadine, both joking and laughing, her hair golden with the dye that covered the gray. He caught a whiff of the orange-blossom smell of the Caron Narcisse Noir perfume that was her favorite scent.

Dear Lord, he missed her! He had forgotten how much until recent events had unearthed buried feelings.

It came to him then that his life need not be the lonely thing it had dwindled into. The remedy was mere paces away. If he entered his own past and contrived to keep his younger self away from a telescope on the night of March 11, 1916, that Norman would never see the six stars vanish, and from that point forward, everything would be different.

Except, not *everything*. In due course, Schmidt would still come to conduct research in Arkham.

Only this time, he would have no companion trying to reach him after a Hound dragged him away.

Besides, much as Norman regretted the disintegration of his marriage, he still could not bear to deny himself the sight of the most extraordinary astronomical phenomenon he had ever witnessed. There were many things he would change if he could, but not that.

With a grunt, he thrust temptation away, and when he did, the sheer statistical improbability of what he had just experienced struck him. If the paths snaked everywhere throughout space-time, what were the odds of stumbling across one that ran to a moment in his own little life?

Steeling himself, he took another look and discovered the scene had changed completely. Now two groups of savages were fighting, or rather, they had been. The ones who resembled the men of Norman's time had gained the upper hand while the short-legged ones with the low, sloping brows were trying to flee. Unfortunately for the Neanderthals, though, victory did not incline the Cro-Magnons to mercy. They chased down their enemies and stabbed them from behind with flint-tipped spears.

Norman suspected that in reality the path had always led to the prehistoric slaughter. Something had tampered with his perception to distract him while it sneaked up on him. With a gasp, he spun around.

The creature stalked on cloven hooves and shaggy legs that bent backward like a goat's hind limbs. From the navel up, it was somewhat less hairy and more manlike, albeit with pointed ears and horns stabbing upward from its brow.

Yet as Norman had feared, it was far different from the satyrs of classical myth. It was nine feet tall, and the non-caprine parts exhibited a burliness more suggestive of an ape than a human being. Scarlet from top to bottom and giving off a butcher-shop stench, it sweat blood, slavered blood, and someone—itself, in some ghastly ritual?—had hammered iron spikes into its eye sockets.

Baring crooked fangs, it roared and lunged.

Norman recoiled, and his foot plunged through empty space. Screaming, arms windmilling, he toppled into the bottomless void.

18

Norman just had time to wonder if, in a realm that existed outside time as human beings normally experienced it, he might live and fall forever. Then he slammed down on his back.

The impact jolted the wind out of him and made him fear he'd injured himself, but when he tried to roll over, he could. He'd landed on a section of the curving path that twisted underneath the intersection.

The satyr peered down from the crossing above, then turned away and disappeared. No doubt it would reappear momentarily when it started down the curved path in pursuit.

Norman's impulse was to flee in the opposite direction. He turned and found that the path he was on only extended several more feet before ending in a convex curve. On the other side waited a white sand beach with blue waves breaking beyond. The directional instinct magic that the incantation had bestowed was like an insistent tap on the shoulder, warning him that the vista before him lay in the wrong direction.

At the moment, however, it might provide a safe haven. Evidently haunters of the curved portions of the maze in the same way the Hounds roamed the angular pathways, the satyrs might be similarly capable of exiting its confines. But Norman's experiences suggested the creatures of Tindalos never ventured far from the breaches, and it seemed a reasonable hypothesis that the horned men didn't either. If so, a dash down the sunlit strand might take him out of danger. If not, perhaps he could hide in the tropical forest that lay inland.

He poised himself to run and then remembered that Stane's magic enabled a mystic to "split the *angle*." What if he ended up in some island wilderness where no one had ever built anything? A place without corners.

Given time, maybe he could create something suitable, but even if so, who was to say a second spell would enable him to navigate his way back to the barn and Arkham? It might only be capable of leading him back to the place from which he embarked. To put it mildly, he didn't understand the sorcery well enough to know one way or the other.

He needed some other way to stay ahead of the satyr. He stepped to the edge of the trail in hopes of spotting another path within jumping distance, preferably an angular one where his pursuer might be unable to follow, but there was nothing but gray void directly below for as far as the eye could see.

The action, however, made the object slung over his shoulder swing and bump against his body, and it was then he recalled he was armed. It angered him that he hadn't remembered sooner, although really it had only been a matter of seconds since the satyr startled him into blundering off the edge of the crossing overhead.

He fumbled the Thompson submachine gun into his trembling hands. At the same instant, the satyr bounded into view and seemed to recognize the threat of the firearm despite the spikes that had put out its eyes. Spraying a mist of bloody spittle, it roared and ran down the curving path.

Norman recalled all that Old Sadie Sheldon himself had taught him about the "trench broom's" Blish lock, "open-bolt" firing position, and what have you. Still, his hands felt clumsy as he sought to cock and point it, as though in a nightmare where a seemingly simple task proved impossible to complete.

At last he was ready to depress the trigger. The gun roared and rattled and, despite the practice he'd put in, the muzzle climbed higher with each round that blazed out of it until he was all but shooting straight up. Unharmed, the satyr charged closer.

Terror screamed for Norman to lower the gun and keep blasting away. Intellect, however, insisted that a shaky novice shooter like himself was unlikely to hit his attacker until it came closer. He forced himself to release the trigger, take a breath, and aim anew.

He resumed firing when the satyr was twenty feet away. This time he did a better job of keeping the submachine gun pointed, and the creature staggered as the rounds slammed into it.

It staggered but wouldn't go down. It kept springing forward, apish hands outstretched to seize its prey.

Norman recalled the breach waiting at his back. Still, hoping he wouldn't take a step too far, he backpedaled as he fired.

The satyr was within three bounds of him. Then two. The trench broom stopped discharging, the 50-round drum depleted.

An instant later, the satyr's hand fell on his shoulder. Fortunately, it then slipped off, leaving a gory streak down his jacket as the creature collapsed.

His heart pounding, Norman gasped for breath. It seemed incredible he'd survived and perhaps even more so that he'd accomplished it by shooting a firearm and killing something monstrous. He hadn't been in so much as a barehanded scuffle since childhood.

Arguably, his victory was cause for optimism. He had just demonstrated he could at least fight the Hounds' allies and prevail if it proved necessary.

But he couldn't find it in himself to celebrate, not when the Hounds themselves were essentially impervious to human weapons, and not when he'd expended an entire magazine's worth of ammunition—half his supply—killing a single satyr. It seemed all too likely he'd run out of cartridges before the labyrinth and the place beyond ran out of horrors.

Still, he'd vowed to go forward, and he would. He loaded fresh ammunition in the drum, reminded himself that if he didn't hold the trigger down, the tommy gun would fire in semiautomatic mode, not expend every last round in a matter of seconds, and he climbed back up toward the scarlet circle and the crossing of curved and angular time.

19

As Norman hiked onward, zigzag trails became more frequent, while the curved ones became less so. At one point, he spied a reptilian form scuttling on a path far to the left and just a hair lower than his own. Although he could now discern that it possessed shorter hind limbs and a dragging tail in addition to the arms he'd observed through the window of Stane's sacrificial chamber, the long neck curling up from the body still made it seem snakelike as much as lizard-like or anthropoid.

The Hound turned, revealing it sensed him as well. He gasped, clutched at the trench sweeper, and had to insist to himself, *Not yet!* The creature was still so distant that he could barely make it out in the ambient gloom.

Perhaps the distance spared him a second skirmish. Maybe the creature mistook him for some ally with the right to travel the maze. Or conceivably, the lack of nearby connecting paths persuaded it to leave his destruction to its fellows. At any rate, after a moment, it continued on its way, and, exhaling, so did he.

Several minutes later, at least according to his faltering sense of the passage of time, he reached a point where angular paths continued to divide and proliferate but none of the curved ones remained for as far as he could see. Instead of merely indicating, his mystical sense of direction now all but tugged him forward like an eager dog on a leash.

Yet other sensations pierced him to offset the feeling of impending arrival. Had he thought about it, he would have said that, except perhaps for interplanetary space, a gulf could scarcely seem more of a void than the emptiness through which he crept. With every step, however, although nothing *looked* different, the feeling of infinite depths intensified. It occurred to him that, whereas before he had been moving through four dimensions, the three conventional ones plus time, now, somehow, he was traversing more than four.

With that realization came a feeling of warning or forbiddance. It seemed a sign he was encroaching on a place that, even more than the labyrinth, was hostile to human existence. Had he been a religious person, he might have taken it for the whisper of a guardian angel imploring him to turn back.

Whatever it was, he declined to heed it, and gradually Tindalos took form in the murk ahead.

=== 20 ===

The Hounds' native realm wasn't like Earth, with its gates into otherness hidden. When Norman looked back, the void and the jagged path he'd just walked were still there in place of the ground and sky the mind expected. The sight of two different realities jammed against one another was enough to make a sane man flinch.

Norman resolved not to look again until he had to. He stared instead at what lay before him.

It was night here. Perhaps it always was. There were no stars visible, so why should there be a sun? A celestial object like a broken moon infested with phosphorescent fungus cast a sickly green light that gleamed on the pyramids and trapezoidal prisms in the distance.

With Norman's departure from the maze, his unnatural sense of direction had dimmed as though it felt it had done the hard work and he should be able to manage the rest himself. Perhaps that meant Schmidt was somewhere in the cluster of buildings, if that was what they were. Hoping it was so, and that the guiding instinct would wake when he needed it once more, the astronomer skulked forward over cracked, barren soil.

Somewhere off to the right, a Hound howled. Norman froze and clutched the tommy gun for a long moment before deciding the cry had come from far away and, more likely than not, had nothing to do with him. Because, so far as he could tell, the call had elicited no reaction from any creature lurking among the angular shapes ahead.

Norman had now crept close enough to make out doorways and windows, confirmation of his initial impression that the masses were buildings, but as yet, he could see neither lights nor motion within. Nor was there anything to hear but the intermittent whisper of the breeze.

Perhaps, for the moment, every Hound was elsewhere. Conceivably they spent most of their time in the labyrinth searching for prey. Dry-mouthed and heart pounding, he made his final approach as stealthily as he could.

Viewed up close, the buildings appeared to be made of charcoal-colored stone polished to a glassy sheen at the edges. To all appearances, the Hounds had carved each from a single huge rock. It was even possible the entire complex was one colossal stone, the seemingly separate pyramids and trapezoidal prisms aboveground could have been extrusions from an even larger mass buried below.

The entryways lacked doors to seal them. The windows were similarly empty, asymmetrical holes without glass, the ones on the ground floors positioned lower than in a human habitation. Norman couldn't have passed beneath them without crawling on hands and knees, so he settled for striding by quickly.

The fetor of the Hounds wafted from doorways and windows alike, a warning that, even if the complex seemed deserted, the creatures might appear at any moment. Norman swallowed repeatedly and bore the stench as best he could. The half-hysterical thought came to him that if he died here, he didn't want to do it with vomit in his beard.

He peered around another corner. Soft blue light shined through the doorway and windows of a smallish pyramid a few yards ahead.

Perhaps Schmidt was inside. If not, maybe Norman was about to get his first really good look at a Hound, a prospect that inspired curiosity and trepidation in equal measure. He skulked forward and peeked in the entrance.

He hadn't found the physicist. He had discovered a Hound, but despite the light, proximity, and the unobstructed view, he still couldn't make out how such creatures looked when intact because the one before him was deep into the process of vivisecting itself.

It lay on the floor in a pool of dark fluids, its wormlike body split lengthwise with the flaps of flesh folded back. Employing its elongated arms, each possessed of two elbows, and the claws at the end of those limbs, it had mostly emptied itself of the organs within and set them around it, and, showing no sign of weakness due to the self-inflicted damage, was busy tearing out the pulsing, twitching tubes and ovoid masses that remained. Its hind legs and tail thumped the floor as the viscera came free.

A long tongue protruded beyond the jagged fangs. Periodically, it writhed toward one of the detached organs and stabbed its pointed tip into it. The proboscis then swelled rhythmically as the musculature inside it worked and matter flowed down what must be a hollow channel at its core. Meanwhile, the punctured organ deflated like a balloon.

Sickened yet fascinated, Norman wondered if he was watching a Hound commit suicide. If Stane had been correct about their regenerative capabilities, quite possibly not. Perhaps the thing could put itself back together or grow new organs to replace the discarded ones.

But if that was the case, what was the purpose of the seeming self-destruction? Was the Hound undertaking a natural part of its life cycle analogous to molting? Performing a ritual of atonement? Doing something that gave it pleasure? In all likelihood, Norman would never know.

The only thing that was clear was that here was additional reason to believe earthly weapons were unlikely to do a Hound any lasting harm. Grateful that the one Hound he'd thus far seen in the complex appeared incapable of harming him—at least until it regenerated or reassembled itself—Norman prowled onward and after another turn discovered Schmidt.

The German lay in the middle of an open space suggestive of a plaza or park with half a dozen stone buildings looming around it. Soil covered all of him except the head in a way that reminded Norman of his daughter burying him in sand at the beach. Schmidt wasn't moving, and in the gloom, his would-be rescuer couldn't tell if he was alive or dead.

Norman hurried toward him. "Schmidt!" he called, keeping his voice low.

To his relief, the physicist rolled his head. He seemed dazed, but that was preferable to deceased.

Norman quickened his stride. "It's me," he said. "I'm going to take you home."

Schmidt's eyes focused, and the slackness in his face gave way to alarm. "No!" he croaked. "Get back!"

An instant later, Norman heard a sibilant, susurrate sound rising from the ground. He looked down. Long, humped ridges in the earth were slithering away from Schmidt and toward him.

They appeared to be burrows with some sort of creature inside. But when one flowed over the toe of his right shoe, he discerned there was nothing there but soil given life or at least the semblance thereof by some unimaginable process. Once it had his foot looped, it hardened.

21

Norman gasped, kicked, and broke the dirt-thing into pieces before it could finish altering its consistency to grip him like concrete. But already, others were trying to coil around his ankles and crawl up his legs. Half tripping with every step, he made a frantic, floundering retreat while resisting the urge to fire the submachine gun at his attackers. He'd likely riddle his own feet if he tried.

He hoped that if he retreated far enough, the dirt-things would break off the pursuit. But there was no sign of it. With every staggering moment that passed, they seemed ever closer to bringing him down. Then they'd surely immobilize him as they had Schmidt. Or simply crush and smother him to death.

He made for a lightless pyramidal building and lunged through the trapezoidal doorway. He swept the Thompson gun from left to right as he looked for new menaces stirring in the gloom.

Nothing. Panting, he turned around.

For the next few seconds, the dirt-things crawled and coiled beyond the threshold that divided ground from stone floor. Eventually they balked and slithered back in Schmidt's direction.

Norman didn't want to step back out of the pyramid. For all he knew, some of the dirt-things had remained to ambush him. He had no way of telling what might be hiding under the surface. But he couldn't help Schmidt from where he was.

He slowly set one foot on the ground. Nothing struck at it. He kept tiptoeing forward until he was close enough to Schmidt for them to converse in low tones. Fortunately, that appeared to leave him outside the circle in which the dirt-things were lurking.

"I never dreamed it was possible for anyone to find me."

"It took some doing,."

"Thank you. But you have to go back if you can. There's nothing you can do for me."

As far as Norman had been able to observe, the dirt-things had no eyes, ears, or noses. It seemed plausible they sensed intruders through vibrations in the ground, and he proposed to give them something to orient on besides his own footfalls. He readied the trench broom and, reminding himself again not to squander ammunition, fired three shots into the earth on the far side of the captive.

A horde of dirt-things writhed away to investigate. Norman ran forward. "Dig your way out!"

He hoped the younger man still had the strength to accomplish something in that regard, but Schmidt merely squirmed to no effect. Norman bent over him to tear at the soil cocoon with his hands.

The dirt bulged into elongated humps, revealing itself to be made of additional creatures. Some crawled over Norman's feet, and many of those he'd diverted with the gunshots were already turning around. He saw no choice but to make a second hasty retreat before he could be snared.

When Norman emerged from the pyramid once more, Schmidt said, "The gun made too much noise! You have to run!"

The sensible part of Norman was in full agreement. As it had before, it assured him he'd already attempted more than any rational person could expect, and no one could blame him if he now gave up.

He pushed that part down and once again did his poor best to imitate Holmes, Raffles, and Boston Blackie. "Don't worry about it," he said. "I have this figured out now." He fired more shots into the ground on the far side of Schmidt. The jolts sent a horde of dirt-things crawling away as they had before.

That still left the ones that had remained with Schmidt, but this time Norman was ready for them. As soon as he reached the German, he fired the submachine gun into the ground, down one side of his body, then the other. Or anyway, he hoped he was missing the physicist's body. It looked like the cocoon pressed Schmidt's arms up against his flanks, but it was impossible to be certain.

The humps of dirt atop and around Schmidt heaved and broke apart. The physicist struggled again to drag himself out of the now-lifeless earth and made a little headway. Norman worked his hands into the soil, managed to grip the younger man under the arms, and pulled until his kicking feet emerged.

Norman glanced around. The rest of the dirt-things had already turned and were crawling back in his and Schmidt's direction.

"Run!" the older man cried, He bolted for the doorway of the stone house that had sheltered him before. Schmidt ran after him.

Norman didn't look around again until he and the German crossed the threshold, and then he saw the ground immediately outside bulging and sliding. By the end of the chase, pursuit had been mere inches behind.

He took a long breath and told himself that it didn't matter by how narrow a margin he and Schmidt had won the race, only that they had. "Are you all right?"

"Thirsty," Schmidt rasped.

In addition to his more destructive military equipment, Norman had brought a canteen. He unscrewed the cap and offered it to the man on the ground. "Go easy at first."

Schmidt took a couple sips, then tilted his head back and drank more deeply.

"The bootlegger from the barn," Norman said. "Do you know what became of him?"

"The things killed him," Schmidt answered, "then threw the

body off the white path into the void."

Norman felt a guilty surge of relief that he needn't attempt to rescue the gangster as well. He scrutinized the patch of earth immediately outside the doorway. The swelling and stirring had subsided. "Then let's go."

Schmidt peered. "Are you certain the things are gone?"

"They didn't linger long before. Once they lost the scent, they crawled back to where their masters stationed them. Anyway, you were right. *We* can't linger here, either. We have to get away."

"Very well, then."

Despite the reassurances he'd just given, it took an effort of will for Norman to shift a foot from the safety of the stone floor to the soil beyond. He held his breath until it was clear that nothing was going to grab him.

He and Schmidt turned in the direction of the maze. At a distance, in the darkness, the boundary where one world met another was invisible, but Norman felt a vacancy even more profound than the starless sky behind and above him.

To his relief, he likewise felt his directional instinct bestirring itself now that he was ready to make the return journey and, although Schmidt had started out hobbling, his stride was growing brisker. The possibility of escape was emerging in him despite whatever torments and privations he'd suffered.

That possibility still seemed the slimmest of hopes. But the two scientists made it out of the complex without any new creatures accosting them.

Was there any chance at all that the noise of the gunfire had failed to rouse the Hounds? After all, they weren't human. They might not even be animals in the truest sense of the term. Perhaps their senses and minds worked in such an alien fashion that the commotion failed to register as cause for action.

It was an encouraging notion while it lasted. Then, however, in the low hills off to the right where Norman had heard the sound before, a Hound howled. An instant later, others answered. An intimation of onrushing malice, like a tidal wave hurtling toward shore, proclaimed that the things were coming.

• • •

— 22 —

"Run!" Norman cried. He suited his actions to his words only to realize moments later that he was outdistancing his companion. His grit and determination notwithstanding, in the wake of his ordeal, Schmidt couldn't keep up.

At least he was running. Norman slowed down to allow the German to catch up and then took care not to leave him behind once more.

Gradually, the gloom ahead turned from black to gray. Like the edge of a sheer cliff, the division between realities appeared and, looking dainty as white threads in the distance, pathways zigzagged out into the void.

"Over there!" Schmidt gasped.

Norman pivoted. One Hound was out in the lead of the pack that Norman could sense charging in its wake. A murkier shadow amid the gloom, it covered ground in bounds that put the satyr he'd encountered to shame.

The fugitives had scant hope of reaching their entry into the labyrinth before the Hound cut them off. Making a little whimpering sound he was helpless to suppress, Norman readied the submachine gun. *Wait until it gets close,* he reminded himself. *Then fire.*

He delayed as long as terror would allow, then began squeezing the trigger. Was he hitting the Hound as it bounded nearer and nearer? He couldn't tell. He certainly wasn't slowing it down.

Perhaps, Norman thought, the only hope was to switch the tommy gun to automatic fire, conserving ammunition be damned. How else was he to inflict enough damage to have *any* hope of keeping the Hound away? He held the trigger down.

The Hound made another leap. Then another. But at the end of the second, it *didn't* immediately spring again. It hesitated a moment, then whirled and scuttled behind a hump in the ground that provided it with cover.

"You hurt it!" Schmidt cried. "You hurt *der Sohn von einem Weibchen!*"

"I doubt I hurt it badly," Norman replied. "It just doesn't feel like taking all the punishment itself when it can just as easily wait for the rest of the pack to catch up. We have to keep moving!"

They ran on.

—— 23 ——

Norman and Schmidt reached the start of the white path ahead of their pursuers but with a chorus of howls ululating at their backs. The calls fell silent as the two men scurried out into the hyper-dimensional chasm that sundered Tindalos from the beginning of curved time.

"Did they give up?" Schmidt panted.

"I doubt it," Norman said. "It's just that we've entered a different aspect of space-time. We'll hear them again when they've crossed the threshold, too."

"Of course," the German said. "I should have inferred as much." He smiled a grim little smile. "I'm not at my best."

"That's understandable." Norman took a drink from his canteen and then gave it to Schmidt.

Schmidt drank and returned the bottle. "How much ammunition do you have left?"

"Only a few rounds, I'm sure. Our one chance is to stay ahead of the pack."

They hurried onward as fast as Schmidt's condition would allow. The physicist was plainly doing the best he could but flagging nonetheless. The reserve of energy he'd tapped when Norman freed him was running low.

Norman felt disgusted with his lack of forethought. He had embarked on this enterprise carrying a submachine gun of all things, yet he had neglected something as basic as food. It was a ghastly joke that he and Schmidt might meet their ends for want of an apple or a Hershey bar.

Still, they reached the portion of the labyrinth where the psychic pressure of infinite depths multiplied beyond the limits of perception abated and curving trails began. Then, however, the howling of the pack rang out behind them. Worse, other Hounds answered the baying from reaches of the labyrinth that still lay ahead.

Schmidt's shoulders slumped. "Perhaps, my friend, if you go on without me—"

"Stop it!" Norman snapped. "We're scientists! We can think our way out of this!" He strained to make good on that declaration. "The Hounds that are after us may or may not recognize me, but they surely have a sense of who you are and where they caught you. If we take the same route back to the barn, they're bound to overtake us. If we make a detour, perhaps we'll throw them off the scent."

Schmidt frowned. "Won't we get lost? Even if we don't, if we take an indirect route, won't the creatures cut us off?"

"There's a great deal I haven't had a chance to tell you. At the moment, I have a sort of compass in my head pointing the way home. As for the rest, do we really know how distance, time, and geometry work in this place? Or how the Hounds think?"

The German grunted. "We do not. Lead on, then."

As Norman took a branching path that snaked to the left and downward, he hoped his homing instinct would prove as accommodating as he'd suggested it would. In truth, he had no way of predicting the capabilities and limitations of the magic, but he'd wanted to sound sure of himself to encourage his companion.

When he and Schmidt descended the "wrong" trail, the directional intuition manifested as the same tap-on-the-shoulder insistence that he reverse course. The sensation remained as the fugitives passed truncated pathways that ran to a stone chamber where men with the heads of snakes huddled over a parchment map, and another to a hilly city on a bay—San Francisco in 1851?—in flames.

Dear Lord, Norman thought, he'd lost his gamble. If he and Schmidt didn't retrace their steps, they'd never find a route back to Arkham; if they did, they were sure to run headlong into the pack. The only viable alternative was to accept exile in a place and era not their own.

He drew breath to confess as much, and then, with a swinging sensation that dizzied him for a moment, the homing instinct realigned itself. However grudgingly, it now pointed forward, not back.

Norman sighed and marched on.

• • •

24

Concerned with shaking the Hounds off the trail, Norman conducted Schmidt through another wrong turn and then another. Each triggered the urging to go back and the attendant anxiety that he'd pushed the magic too hard and broken it, or that he'd blundered down a path from which it would prove impossible to reach the barn. Fortunately, on both occasions, after a minute or so, the compass needle inside his head pivoted in deference to his decisions.

The Hounds bayed from time to time, but as best he could determine there were no longer several howling from the same spot. Apparently the pack had dispersed to seek the fugitives down various paths. Perhaps that was grounds for hope that his evasive tactic had done some good.

He needed that to be the case, for at the moment, neither Schmidt nor his aging, sedentary rescuer could muster the vigor to press on faster than a quick walk. Norman supposed that meant they could spare the breath to whisper back and forth. At least that way, even if worst came to worst, he and his fellow scientist would perish with their curiosity satisfied.

"Do you know," he asked, "why the creatures took you alive and held you captive in Tindalos?"

"'Tindalos?'"

"The name of their world. Possibly."

"Ah. Well, no, truly, I don't know why they took me prisoner. Except…you realize the brutes are in some measure telepathic?"

Norman thought of how he had sensed Hounds spying from the other sides of corners and the manner in which an element of their howling bypassed the ears to stab straight inside the head with a filthy intimacy. Presumably those phenomena were examples of one mind brushing another. "I suppose so."

"Well, after the one that captured me dragged me home, a dozen of them clustered around me and all dug into my thoughts at once. I don't know what they were looking for, or why. I wasn't able to see into *their* heads. But it wasn't pleasant. I…" Schmidt swallowed. "After I while, I wasn't myself anymore."

"I can imagine," Norman said, although he couldn't, entirely, and for that he was glad.

"After that was over, they left me alone. Buried like a dog buries a bone to dig up and eat later, I imagine." Schmidt laughed in a way that reminded Norman of Stane.

The astronomer gripped the younger man's shoulder. "Hang on. You're away from them now, and we have to be quiet so you can keep away."

Schmidt nodded. "Of course. Forgive me, and tell me how you managed to come for me. The story will keep me from dwelling on things I shouldn't think about."

Perhaps it would even though it too centered on the Hounds. Norman related it as he and Schmidt hurried along watching for shapes and movement ahead, behind, and on nearby paths.

Toward the end of his account, the homing instinct became a veritable pull to indicate he was nearing his destination. This time, he followed straight where it led.

The other pathways blurred and faded. After several more steps, only the one he and Schmidt were traversing remained, zig-zagging up to a right-angle notch of an endpoint. He sensed the barn beyond.

Something in his manner must have communicated his elation. Schmidt asked, "Is that the way home?"

"Yes!" Norman answered. He hurried forward.

"Wait!" the physicist cried.

For a moment, Norman didn't know why Schmidt was alarmed. Then he felt what the younger man had: the malevolent scrutiny of an entity just out of view.

The Hound didn't remain that way for long. Perhaps it had lurked in hiding until its prey ventured close, but now, sweating bluish slime, eyes like black pearls staring, it sprang out of nothingness onto the trail to block the doorway back to Earth.

═══ 25 ═══

Norman opened fire. The Hound snarled as the bullets struck but stalked forward anyway, as though the wounds were as inconsequential as gnat stings. After a few seconds, the tommy gun clacked empty.

Now there was no choice but to flee, or at least he imagined so for an instant. But as he turned, howling sounded at his back. The rest of the pack was closing in fast. If he and Schmidt turned tail, they'd simply run into the creatures.

Norman felt a surge of emotion. For a moment, he mistook it for a recurrence of the terror that had so often afflicted him of late. But it wasn't. Here at the end of his race, with the normal human world just yards away but out of reach nonetheless, fear had given way to anger.

Blast it, it wasn't fair that he'd dared and endured so much only to have it come to nothing! He could die, he surely would die, but he wasn't going to fail. Schmidt had to get away.

"Here's what we're going to do," Norman said. "I'll advance to meet the thing. Provoke it into focusing its attention on me. When it attacks, you dash past it and on through the breach." He just had to hope that, even though he was the one who'd cast the spell of opening, Schmidt would be able to pass through from this side without him.

"No," said Schmidt.

"Don't be quixotic. It's better that one of us live than neither, and if that's the best we can achieve, logic indicates it should be the young genius with a bright future before him. Now do as I told you."

Norman took a deep breath and walked forward, and, seemingly in no hurry, savoring the moment, the Hound prowled toward him. Its neck curved like a question mark to counterbalance the crocodilian head stretched out far ahead of the rest of its body. Its tongue writhed through its jagged fangs, and its stench suffused the air.

"Well," said Norman, "what are you waiting for?" He raised the Thompson gun to club the creature with the butt end.

Unfortunately, he didn't get the chance. The Hound reared and backhanded him, swinging one forelimb in such a way that the claws didn't pierce or rend him. Everything shattered into confusion, and when he came to his senses, he no longer had hold of the weapon and was lying on his back with the creature crouching over him.

The long tongue writhed at him. The Hound touched the point to Norman's forehead, then poised it before his right eye, then pressed it lightly against his throat, as if playing with its now-helpless prey. Then, seemingly tiring of the game, it plunged the needle-sharp member into its prey's shoulder and began to suck his blood.

The pain was hideous. Norman thrashed and battered futilely with his fists.

Then the Hound's body hitched to the side. Schmidt was pushing on it. He hadn't fled to safety after all, merely waited until the Hound was distracted to launch an attack.

Unfortunately, the effort had accomplished nothing. The creature had only shifted position slightly, and now, slipping its proboscis out of Norman's flesh for the moment, it twisted to bring its jaws to bear.

As it turned, though, Schmidt's hand slid in the Hound's coating of slime, and his finger jabbed into one of its round little eyes. The creature flinched and faltered. Injury and the attendant pain couldn't truly stop it, but they could balk and fluster it for an instant.

"Push it again!" Norman shouted. "Fast!" He scrambled to his knees, planted his hands on the Hound's body, and shoved. With both men pushing, the beast lurched sideways off the edge of the path and toppled into the gulf.

The sudden absence of resistance made Schmidt stagger forward to the brink. As he teetered, Norman threw his arms around the younger man's legs, anchoring him until he regained his balance.

Afterward, Norman peered over the side. He half expected to see that, as he himself had done when the satyr surprised him into a fall, the Hound had landed on a path just a few yards down and was even now rallying to hunt its prey anew. But there was nothing but gray emptiness directly below for as far as he could see.

=== **26** ===

"Are you all right?" panted Schmidt.

Norman inspected his shoulder wound. It was deep, but it wasn't spurting. The Hound hadn't punctured an artery. "I'll survive" he said, standing up and applying pressure with his hand. "What about you?"

"I'm all right, too."

"Then let's move." As they hurried up the path, Norman added, "You should have done as I told you."

"Are you truly complaining?"

Norman smiled. "Well, maybe not as such."

With Hounds baying in the maze behind him, the two scientists stepped from the end of the path back into the barn. The whiskey-scented space was dark. Norman had been gone long enough for day to turn to night.

He felt, or imagined he felt, a slight, sourceless trembling that reminded him of being in proximity to Doyle Jeffries's printing presses. It made him hesitate for an instant, and then he decided that in all likelihood he was simply feeling his own shakiness, brought on by fear, exhaustion, and the shock of his injury. In any case, there was no time to stand and puzzle over the source of the sensation.

"Wait just a moment," he said, then stooped, groped, and found the bundle of dynamite. He lit a match and then the fuse which, once it flared to life, provided a bit of illumination. "Blow up the corner and you destroy the doorway. Or at least I hope so."

"Look," said Schmidt. He sounded ill.

Norman turned. The debris on the floor was shivering. After another second, the shaking became forceful enough for scraps of wood and pieces of broken glass to clink together.

"The Dholes," he said, feeling sick himself. He should have remembered the Hounds had one more ally and thus potentially one last trick to play.

Something immense and vermiform, distantly related to the Hounds, perhaps, exploded up from the center of the floor and, coated in sludge, swayed back and forth. All but featureless beneath its mask of muck, its head brushed and bumped the rafters as it seemingly took its bearings.

The creature would orient on one of them in another moment, and it had better be the one who had the desperate idea of how to contend with it. Norman pulled a stick of dynamite from the bundle awaiting the touch of the flame crawling up the fuse. Then, sidestepping along the wall, he shouted. "Look at me!"

The huge head swiveled, tracking him. The mouth opened wide, clearly discernible now despite the gloom and the curtain of slime dripping over it.

Norman took out the fresh matchbook he'd procured for this expedition and struck a match. He started to touch the flame to the dynamite as the Dhole's head hurtled down at him.

He flung himself aside and just avoided the enormous creature's jaws. Unfortunately, the frantic evasion blew out the match.

More quickly than anything so huge should be able to recover, the Dhole reared, oriented on him, and struck at him a second time. Once again, he barely managed to keep the thing from snatching him up in its jaws.

He faked a sidestep left and then dodged right instead. That confused the Dhole long enough for him to strike a match and set the entire matchbook burning. Surely that much fire wouldn't blow out!

The Dhole struck. He lurched out of the way and, teeth clenched against the pain of the flame searing his fingers, touched the burning matchbook to the dynamite's remaining nub of fuse. It caught, and he threw the explosive. The Dhole was huge enough and the barn sufficiently spacious that he hoped to land it where it would hurt the creature but not Schmidt or himself. With luck, its body would actually shield them from the blast.

The enormous head descended at him, and then the stick exploded. The Dhole flew into convulsions that hurled wood and glass through the air and crashed portions of its bulk against the walls.

In this confined space, the gigantic worm was scarcely less dangerous in the throes of agony than when trying to kill. Norman retraced his steps and found Schmidt scurrying along the wall to meet him. They hurried onward together.

A flying piece of crate bashed Norman on the hip. A second later, his peripheral vision revealed something huge hurtling in his direction. He recoiled, jerking Schmidt back with him and, charred and torn by the grenades, the Dhole's tail slammed into the wall and smashed a section outward.

The two scientists ducked through the hole and rushed on to the Bearcat. The roadster was halfway down the drive when the bundle of dynamite exploded and blew out the southwest corner of the barn.

Schmidt's better judgment told him to keep moving, but he found he had to see what would happen next. He pulled the brake lever and twisted around in his seat for a better look.

Quicker than he would have imagined, leaping yellow flame engulfed the barn. Perhaps the spilled liquor provided an accelerant. In any case, nothing enormous and wormlike was crawling out of the conflagration. Still shaky with adrenaline but somewhat reassured nonetheless, he drove on.

"Good," Norman said. "The hard part's done."

Schmidt peered at him. "What's the easy part?"

"Stane believed the sites on your list form a sort of pattern that makes it easy for the Hounds to find their way to Arkham. By that logic, if the pattern ceases to exist, it will spoil their road map. Well, we've already made a start, and thanks to some checking I did at the *Advertiser*, I know three of the other locations are empty houses. I have cans of gasoline in the trunk, and I intend to finish the evening with a little arson."

═ 27 ═

When Schmidt and Norman entered the Science Department, colleagues clustered around to congratulate the physicist on being found safe and sound—give or take—and the astronomer on discovering him lost and disoriented in a patch of woods west of town.

It seemed to Norman there was something tentative about the felicitations that came his way. Probably people still thought it odd that he had ever lost track of the eminent visitor in the first place, and they might well find the whole fabricated sequence of events— the chance fall, the concussion, wandering off in confusion, and all the rest of it—peculiar.

Surely Doyle Jeffries did. The journalist knew the derelict houses that had burned were locations on the physicist's list. But in lieu of any better explanation, he had printed the two scientists' account as they'd provided it.

Norman found the approbation of his fellow faculty members, uncertain though it might be, pleasant. A part of him would have been happy to linger and savor it, but that bit was no match for the imperative that had driven him for a decade, and when the two of them could manage it politely, he shepherded Schmidt to his office.

Schmidt peered into the corners before entering. His ordeal had left him haggard and jumpy, Norman hoped not permanently so.

He too was prone to start at shadows and unexpected noises and bolt awake from nightmares. Yet paradoxically, when residual fear was not nagging, he felt surprisingly well. As though the hellish episode had been good for him.

He removed the books and journals from the extra chair so Schmidt could avail himself of it. Then he set a stack of notes and astronomical photographs in front of him.

"This is everything that might be relevant," Norman said. "The rest—," he waved his hand to indicate the remaining contents of the office, bookmarks, Moore Push-Pins, and all, "—amounts to false leads, all of it."

He all but held his breath as Schmidt went through the material. At length the German looked up and said, "I'm sorry. All you did for me, and in the end, I don't have anything for you."

It was disappointing, but not, Norman realized, as bitter a blow as it might once have seemed. "That's all right. I appreciate you trying."

"So what becomes of us now, my friend? Are we safe?"

Norman shrugged. "In theory, a Hound could emerge from any corner anywhere and anytime, but under normal conditions, it's not something that happens often. If destroying the pattern threw them off our scent, we should be fine. Of course, you change your odds if you go searching for discontinuities again."

Schmidt shivered. "Not likely. Yet we made incredible discoveries. If they don't amount to an entirely new paradigm, they come close. There must be some safe way to study them." He smiled for an instant. "And to pursue such research without the scientific community deciding the researcher is hopped up."

It was good to hear the physicist slip into American slang. It seemed a promising sign for his eventual recovery. "Good luck with that."

"What about you? Will you keep chasing the mystery of the missing stars?"

"Yes." But he would try to keep obsession from isolating him as it had before. His students and colleagues deserved better of him.

He deserved it of himself.

"Do you know how?"

Norman thought of the *Livre d'Eibon* and the six volumes of Stane's notes sitting in his bookcase at home. "I have an idea."

About the Author

Richard Lee Byers is the author of over forty fantasy and horror novels including *Pathfinder Tales: Called to Darkness*, *Blind God's Bluff: A Billy Fox Novel*, *The Reaver: The Sundering Book IV*, *Black Dogs* (first in his new "Black River Irregulars" trilogy), *The Ghost in the Stone*, and the books in the "Impostor" series. His novel T*he Spectral Blaze* won Diehard GameFAN's award for the Best Game-Based Novel of 2011.

Richard has also published dozens of short stories, some of which are collected in the e-books *The Q Word and Other Stories* and *Zombies in Paradise*. *The Fate of All Fools*, his first graphic novel, is now available, and he is also working on new electronic games.

Richard lives in the Tampa Bay area and is a frequent guest at Gen Con, Dragon Con, and Florida SF conventions. He invites everyone to follow him on Twitter @rleebyers, friend him on Facebook, and add him to their Circles on Google+.

PRICE FIVE CENTS

MISSING SCIENTIST FOUND ALIVE

ARKHAM — Last night, Professor Claus Schmidt of the University of Berlin was found alive in the countryside west of Arkham after having disappeared for days.

A physicist and protégé of Albert Einstein, Professor Schmidt was visiting Arkham to conduct research. On the night of the 17th, his investigations led him and a colleague, Professor Norman Withers of Miskatonic University, to a seemingly abandoned farm west of the city. There, they discovered bootleggers had used the barn to warehouse Canadian whiskey.

Undeterred, Schmidt and Withers set about their research and became separated. Eventually, Withers realized that Schmidt had disappeared. He searched his immediate environs, failed to find his colleague, and reported the matter to the Miskatonic County Sheriff's Office.

Sheriff Engle and his fellow officers undertook a comprehensive search of the area the following morning. They, too, failed to find any trace of Professor Schmidt.

In the days that followed, Professor Withers continued searching on his own. Eventually, he discovered Schmidt in a patch of woods near the farm. Schmidt had been wandering lost and disoriented since falling and suffering a blow to the head.

Professor Withers drove Schmidt to St. Mary's Hospital, where physicians treated him for exposure and exhaustion before releasing him into the custody of his colleague.

ROUND-THE-WORLD FLYERS LAND IN SAN DIEGO

who completed

NEW
RY

will soon
rs—that is
r to seeing
clarity.
ean of the
ce Depart-
witz, along
sident James
the impres-
ceremonial
d of directors
elped to host
mony, which
dents, faculty,
Sadie Sheldon's
, without a doubt
lamented the
ooden chapel,
cupied the site
Erwin reassured
school has the
eligion Depart-
ue to look to the
his spot."
st patiently wait
servatory, we can
he project's future
air. After several
e university with-
little to no expla-
f the project was
ntil the remaining
sly donated by an
r. "We are eternally
ervatory's guardian
kowitz. "Were it not
would remain stuck
glimpse the furthest
Way."
the free-standing
equipped with one
in the global sci-

WHAT KIND OF RESEARCH?

WHY HIDE THAT FROM US?

AGAIN, WHAT KIND OF PHYSICS RESEARCH DO YOU DO ON AN OLD FARM IN THE MIDDLE OF THE NIGHT?

DID YOU AND SCHMIDT SAMPLE THE MERCHANDISE, WITHERS?

DOES THAT FIGURE IN SOMEHOW?

BECAUSE EVERYONE BLAMED YOU, WITHERS?

EVEN THOUGH THE DEPUTIES HAD ALREADY SEARCHED THERE?

BUT NOT A CONCUSSION OR ANY KIND OF HEAD INJURY?

THIS WHOLE STORY IS OBVIOUS BUSHWA EVEN IF YOU IGNORE THE COINCIDENCE OF THE BARN AND THREE OF THE EMPTY HOUSES ~~BURNING DOWN~~ THE SAME NIGHT SCHMIDT WAS FOUND.

SOMEDAY, WITHERS, YOU'RE GOING TO NEED ANOTHER FAVOR, AND THEN I'M GOING TO PRY THE REAL STORY OUT OF YOU.

FARMER VANISHES

ARKHAM – Christian Roberts, a farmer whose property lies adjacent to the Aylesbury Pike, disappeared yesterday. According to his wife, Agatha, he went into the barn at approximately 9:00 a.m. and has not been seen or heard from since. The Miskatonic County Sheriff's Office has begun a search of the farm and the surrounding area, but thus far the sheriff has found no sign of him.

Remarkably, this is not the first such misfortune to befall the Roberts family. After entering the same barn on November 16, 1871, Samuel Roberts, Christian's father, vanished, never to be seen again.

Asked for comment, Mrs. Roberts said tearily, "I've always worried that whatever took my husband's father was still lurking around. From time to time, I thought I felt it watching. I urged Christian to sell the place, but he refused. I am not ...... will become of us now."

SCHOOLBOYS MISSI

ARKHAM – William Harris, age Philip Schuyler, 11, have been ed missing after failing to attend Thursday morning.

The two boys are frequent truants. their failure to show up for class, deemed regrettable, was not regard cause for alarm. When they did not to their family homes by nightfall, he er, their parents contacted the autho In due course, the Arkham City Department began a search for the ing children, but to date, their efforts proved unavailing.

Although police spokesmen declin comment on the ongoing investiga the Gazette has learned a witness obse the boys entering South Church Ceme at approximately 3:00 p.m. on Thurs afternoon. It does not appear that any saw them come out again.

South Church Cemetery has a history unexplained disappearances. On Octo 11, 1845, Hezekiah Whipple, a sexton ging a grave, vanished with the task completed, and on June 19, 1889, A Palmer, a widow who had come to pla flowers on her late husband's headsto never re-emerged from the cemetery.

Dertig

ISKATONIC RIVER VALLEY

EMBER 23, 1924

RUDER MURDERS BARBARA MATHEWS, MUTILATES JONATHON HOBART STANE

KHAM – At approximately 10:00 st night, an intruder entered the family residence on Powder Mill attacked Jonathon Hobart Stane Barbara Mathews, and fled. Miss ews was pronounced dead at the Mr. Stane survived, but St. Mary's ital, where he is currently a patient, his condition as "grave."

ter Congress declared war on April r. Stane was one of the first Arkham to enlist in the Army. He was due to rt for duty in Boston on the 15th, and nd Miss Mathews were enjoying a fi-vening together before he caught the n. He had given household staff the at off.

hough police have yet to find signs of ed entry, an intruder found his way the house. He then attacked Miss thews and Mr. Stane with a large blade, sibly a Bowie knife. Stabbed through heart, Miss Mathews perished.

Though wounded, Mr. Stane survived. lice conjecture that he fought the at-ker off with a cavalry saber, a memen-of his late father's service in Theodore osevelt's Rough Riders. After the in-der fled, Mr. Stane made his way to a ephone and called for help before col-osing.

It appears nothing was stolen. Still, Chief Adams deems it "unlikely" the kill-er was motivated by personal animus. He considers it more probable that Mr. Stane and Miss Mathews surprised a burglar who then lashed out and ultimately fled in a panic, abandoning the prizes for which he came.

Certainly, there is no obvious reason for anyone to harbor malice toward either of the victims. Active in church and civic affairs, young Mr. Stane is a philanthropist whose generosity has benefitted Miska-tonic University and many other Arkham institutions. The daughter of a prominent Kingsport family, Miss Mathews enjoyed a similarly sterling reputation.

Chief Adams assures the citizens of Arkham that "the manhunt is ongoing and this monster will be caught." He also urges anyone with information about the case to contact his department immediately.

Los Angeles, California
August 9, 1921

My dear Norman,

This is the most difficult letter I have ever had to write.

You ask me again to come home, and it breaks my heart to say no because I still love you. Or at least, I love the man you were before that damnable night changed everything.

Please believe me when I say I was always proud of your work and the zeal you brought to it. I never begrudged you the nights you spent away from me peering through a telescope. Not until your great discovery.

And afterward, it did not matter that no one else believed. I believed in you. I had faith that eventually you would be proved right, and if not, well, so be it. I married you, not your scientific reputation.

But, Norman, you broke in the face of all the doubt and derision. Or perhaps I am not giving you enough credit. Perhaps it was true scientific curiosity that kept you digging away at your mystery.

Either way, it does not matter. As the months and years passed, you became more and more obsessed until I barely saw you anymore. Honestly, I am surprised you even noticed when I left.

From your infrequent letters—so terse it would be more accurate to call them notes—it is clear nothing has changed, nor is anything likely to. That is why I am filing for divorce.

Now you are wondering how to change my mind. You cannot. Oh, maybe if you dropped everything, caught the next train to Los Angeles, courted me like when we were in college, but you will not.

Perhaps you will think about it. But in the end, the lure of your precious observatory will prove too strong. You will tell yourself that you have too much pride to beg or that it would not have worked anyway.

And so, my love, goodbye. I hope you find your vanished star.

Bernadine

985 Sandusia
Chicago, Illinois

ary 2, 1917

Professor Withers:

I regret to inform you that we are rejecting your article "On the
overy and Subsequent Disappearance of Six Stars in the Vicinity of Canis
r."

Perhaps it would be the course of discretion to let it go at that,
until now, you have been a valued contributor to this journal. You and I
spoken cordially at various conferences. Thus, as a well-wisher—if not a
se friend—I feel moved to explain the rejection in the hope my candor will
re you frustration and embarrassment later on.

Frankly, the paper dismayed me. I would have deemed it a poor effort
it come from an undergraduate. Penned by a full professor of Astronomy at
restigious university, it is astonishing verging on inexcusable.

Surely you understand our discipline depends on observations and
eriments capable of replication. Without these, there is no science. What,
n, is one to make of your claim to have sighted six uncatalogued stars
at vanished almost immediately thereafter? What are your fellow astronomers
pposed to do with such an assertion? It reads less like sober research
an a fantastic tale from a pulp magazine, especially when one considers
e distances involved. What phenomenon could eclipse each of these widely
parated bodies in a matter of moments, only to disappear itself thereafter
thoroughly that no trace of it remains detectable?

I put it to you: is it not more plausible that you have been deceived
meteors burning up in the atmosphere, lightning, foreign matter on the lens
your instrument, and/or eyestrain attendant upon overwork? The answer is
ovious.

As a colleague who desires only the best for you, I encourage you to
ake a good long rest. Then, put this rubbish behind you and return to real
stronomy. Should you do so, it will be my pleasure to consider your subse-
uent papers for publication.

Yours sincerely,

Carl Yancy, Ph.D

130   120

α
Sirius
β

CANIS MAJOR

The six-
fingered
hand?

Degarmo's wrinkled face so sagged that it seemed about to slide off his skull like molten wax, and his sparse white hair bristled like tufts of dry, dead grass.

I liked it that he was a goblin of a man. It made me feel less freakish. My face was still bandaged from the final surgery, but the doctors had warned me what to expect when the wrapping came off.

Not that I was dwelling on Degarmo's appearance or my own. That was only a passing thought. Mainly, I was hoping he could save me.

Degarmo removed the bundles of banknotes one by one from the briefcase and riffled through them until my patience ran out. "It is all there," I said.

He smiled as if the actual goal of the examination had been to provoke me into an outburst. "Yes," he said, "I believe it is. Come with me."

With that, he led me out of the dusty, cluttered study, up narrow, groaning stairs, and ultimately into the old house's garret. The windows were shuttered, but a trapezoidal skylight provided a view of the night sky.

In the corner dangled the skeleton of one who, in life, must have been as deformed as Joseph Merrick the Elephant Man himself, with a skull as doglike as it was human and claws at the ends of massive finger bones. Painted geometric designs adorned the walls, floor, and even portions of the ceiling, and the tang of some bitter incense lingered in the air.

"Stand there," Degarmo said, pointing, "and keep quiet."

I did as instructed. He picked up a book bound in cracked, crumbling blue leather, positioned himself under the skylight, and began to read aloud. I did not recognize the language. It so often hissed or croaked that it scarcely sounded like actual speech at all.

The painted designs began to rotate and then to revolve around one another. It frightened me, dizzied me, and made me sick to my stomach. I reminded myself I had sought out Degarmo for this, for the uncanny, and bore up as best I could.

When he finished reading, seething shadow streamed down through the skylight as if the glass was not there. Taller than it was wide, and twice as tall as Degarmo, the inky cloud swirled before him. The garret became icy cold, and I clenched my jaw to keep my teeth from chattering.

"It has been some time," whispered the darkness. "I wondered whether you regretted our bargain."

"I simply did not require your services," Degarmo replied. "Not until now."

"What would you have?"

Degarmo gestured to me. "This man survived an encounter with something from beyond, but he believes it is coming back for him. He needs protection."

Though the dark thing had no face or eyes, I felt its attention fix on me. The scrutiny pierced me as if I were a butterfly in a collector's display case.

Finally the entity's regard swung back to Degarmo. "You seek my destruction," it said, "to escape the consequences of our pact."

The old man blinked. "Why would you say that?"

"You hope to pit me against the Hounds. The other human carries their mark."

"I do not even know what that means." Degarmo took a breath. "But I do know you and I have a pact, and you are bound to do as I command."

"I was never 'bound.' For my own reasons, I indulged you. That indulgence has reached an end."

The cloud leaped forward and engulfed the old man. Half obscured amid the darkness, he floated upward to dangle helplessly as something akin to invisible claws ripped his clothing and the flesh beneath. His screams echoed.

I whirled toward the stairs. Then I remembered Degarmo's knowledge had been my only chance. He was lost to me now, dying before me, but the knowledge remained in the form of the blue book, dropped when the darkness scooped him up.

I crept to the foot of the shadow. Trembling, holding my breath, I reached, and, perhaps utterly intent on killing Degarmo, the shadow thing did not pay me any mind.

I grabbed the book and bolted.

Monday, May 12th, 1919

Attempting to make sense of the blue book—the *Livre d'Eibon*, to give it its proper title—is the most difficult task I have ever undertaken. Fortunately, I studied French in school. Unfortunately, I studied modern French, not this archaic version.

And language is not even the chief obstacle. Often the author—a wizard of lost Atlantis, or so he claims—assumes knowledge I do not possess. Sometimes he speaks in metaphor and allegory, and periodically the text seems to descend into pure gibberish like the ravings of a madman.

Yet I persevere. Somehow, I know the beast is not done with me, and what other hope do I have? At least, having seen Degarmo's shadow creature, I know the book contains real magic if I can but puzzle it out.

Gradually, a few truths have yielded themselves to rational understanding, while more seemed to creep into—to poison, perhaps—my subconscious. Ever since the attack, I have suffered nightmares, but hitherto, they invariably centered on the creature that maimed me. I still have plenty of those, but now I also see Eibon's Atlantis, the abominations its priests perpetrated to honor its god, and the act of mercy that turned that deity against it. I glimpse a king in an ivory mask and yellow tatters, and colossal eel-like things that, shunning light and warmth, swim in black voids far from any star.

The visions are terrifying, but perhaps they are useful as well. Today, having extricated myself from my tangled, sweat-sodden bed sheets and shuffled back to my desk, I opened the blue book to discover an illustration and a passage I had never seen before, even though I have by now leafed through the volume a hundred times.

Did the book hide certain pages until it deemed me ready to see them? Did it physically transform?

It matters not. I care only about what has been revealed. The illustration is of my nemesis the beast—or one of its kind, anyway—and the accompanying text expounds on the nature of the creatures.

Degarmo's familiar called them "Hounds," and Eibon expands the name to the "Hounds of Tindalos," although who or what Tindalos is remains unclear. Evidently, the things can appear anytime and anywhere, and when they do, it is to hunt human prey. Like vampires, they drain us of our blood before vanishing as mysteriously as they came.

If there is any defense against them, the passage does not mention it. It does say that, just as my instincts warned me, in the rare instances when a man initially escapes, the Hound comes back for him sooner or later.

For someone in my situation, that sounds like cause for despair, but I will not give up! I shall go on learning until I find an answer!

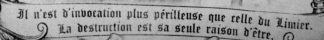

Il n'est d'invocation plus périlleuse que celle du Limier.
La destruction est sa seule raison d'être.

QUEL EST LE NOM DE...

Beware the maze. ev'ry path is p'rilous. but if't be true thee might not but venture th're, keepeth to the curves.

Wednesday, September 17th, 1920

After witnessing Degarmo's death, I had little inclination to seek out other self-styled experts in the occult. But the time came when I could glean no further information from the *Livre d'Eibon*. It might be there, but either I had reached the limits of my capacity to comprehend it, or the book itself was thwarting me for its own unfathomable reasons.

In desperation, I had my private detective make further inquiries. His discoveries led me to a used bookshop in Greenwich Village.

Slight of build, bespectacled, and of a bookish appearance in general, Mr. Chubinsky—the proprietor—was exactly what one might have expected. The assistant was not. Burly and scowling, he looked like a hoodlum and acted the part when he patted me down.

"Was that necessary?" I asked.

"The books are priceless," Chubinsky replied. "You would not be the first to try to steal them. Come—I will take you to them."

Whereupon he and the guard escorted me into the basement.

Most of the space was given over to the storage of books presumably even less salable than those gathering dust upstairs. But at the back of the cellar, a chair and table sat in the harsh glow of a bare bulb, and atop the table reposed three volumes of a different sort.

"No reading out loud," Chubinsky said. "Otherwise, MacGrath here will shoot you on the spot."

"You truly are afraid of the harm these books could do."

"You should be, too."

"Yet you rent them out to anyone who has the cash."

Chubinsky grinned, a leer that transformed his mild countenance into something wolfish and malign. "I did not say I did not want them doing harm. I simply do not want to be there when it happens. I will leave you to it."

The three books were *Cultes des Goules, De Vermiis Mysteriis,* and the *Pnakotic Manuscripts.* An anonymous scholar had translated the latter from Greek into English, and so I began with the material in my native tongue.

It was a happy choice. Halfway through, I found a description of something called "the Maze" along with an artist's attempt to depict it.

The Maze is supposedly a network of pathways running through a kind of Limbo. A traveler can use them to journey to any point in space and time, but not without danger. Hostile creatures prowl the trails, particularly the "angular" ways.

Time, it seems, is of two sorts, curved and angular, and the latter paths run all the way to the beginning of everything, when all time was jagged and sharp. That primordial epoch was called—or associated with something called—"Tindalos."

I understand almost nothing of this. Yet perhaps it is the lifeline I need, or at least a strand of it. Perhaps it will help me survive.

Friday, October 3rd, 1920

I inserted the glass eye. Despite all the surgery, the pressure hurt the empty socket. I then applied the theatrical makeup. I had been practicing for weeks and did an adequate job of covering the scars. Still, the results looked wrong in the mirror, if not instantly fraudulent, lumpy and blemished.

Fortunately, it would be dark, and I did not need to look like Rudolph Valentino. I only had to avoid making strangers recoil in alarm.

I topped off my disguise with eyeglasses and a fedora, then made my way through the house. With its new curved molding and closed doors, the place was as safe as I could make it, but I still jumped at any creak or shifting shadow. I could never make my home entirely safe, and that was the point of tonight's excursion.

Once I was behind the wheel of my Peerless Model 56 and left Arkham for open countryside, I felt more at ease. The interior of the car was not completely devoid of angles, but it seemed unlikely a Hound would suddenly burst into the confines of a moving vehicle.

Anxiety returned when I reached Boston, where angles were everywhere. I did not know whether I was more worried about that or my ability to successfully commit the crime I intended.

Not far from Central Square was a narrow street with a speakeasy at one end of a particular block. The other street-level establishments were unassuming storefronts, closed at this time of night, some with derelicts sitting or lying in the doorways.

Circling the block, I spotted a vagrant slumped in one such refuge all alone, with no witnesses close at hand. I parked, climbed out of the car, and approached him.

Dirty with a shaggy beard, he peered at me, started to speak, and then hesitated. Something about me put him off.

I pulled a folded ten-dollar bill from my breast pocket and showed it to him. "There's supposed to be a speak around here somewhere," I said, "but I'll be damned if I can find it. I'll give you this if you show me where it is."

He considered me anew, and perhaps my expensive clothes,

luxurious car, and apparent dimwitted helplessness reassured him—the speakeasy was, after all, only a couple hundred feet away. At any rate, I no longer seemed dangerous. Given my readiness to dispense extravagant tips for essentially nothing, I seemed the answer to a derelict's prayers.

"Sure, mister," he slurred, "I'll show ya."

I ushered him into the Model 56, and the unwashed stink of him filled the enclosed space. Trying not to show my disgust, I offered him a drink from the drugged flask, and he gulped it down. Seconds later, he was snoring.

I had worried that I would feel guilty by now, but so far, so good. I felt only a sort of gloating contempt for a victim who had let himself be taken so easily. Well, that and hope that my scheme would work.

Back home again, I closed the garage door to ensure that no one would see me lift the derelict from the car and carry him into the house. I put him in the cell and locked him in.

Then I chanted the incantation. The snarling, yipping words were difficult, sometimes painful to recite, and since I had never spoken the whole thing straight through before, start to finish, I could not know whether it would work properly.

It did. Looking through the little barred window in the door, I saw the painted glyphs on the wall pulse and glow. Then, I caught a whiff of a Hound's fetor. My nerve failed me, and I backed away.

Thus, I did not see the slaughter. I only heard the howl, the sucking, and the derelict's screams when violation roused him from his stupor.

When the cell fell silent, I mustered the courage to return to the window. The Hound had carried my offering back into its own realm and hadn't lingered to finish killing me.

I still feel no remorse, only satisfaction and relief. I know now I will make many such sacrifices in the coming years, each extending my own life a little longer.

I t feels vaguely odd to record my thoughts in the same journal the maniac who tried to murder me used to record his. Yet, the final volume has unfilled pages. Stane's studies have now become my own. So why not?

I emerged from my adventure—such a jolly word for such terrifying experiences!—a changed man. In retrospect, I see that obsession was shriveling me into an embittered travesty of the person I formerly was. Something about my ordeal woke me from my decline, and I have promised myself not to lapse into another.

Still, it would be false to claim I am any less intent on my goal than before. If anything, the opposite is true. For the drawing in the *Livre d'Eibon* is the first new evidence to come my way since the night I made my original observations.

Many would disagree that it does, in fact, constitute evidence. Yet, the hand in the picture is reaching for stars, and it has six fingers. Surely that is more than coincidence, and I now know firsthand that phenomena most would dismiss as the stuff of superstition can turn out to be frighteningly real. So, without losing sight of accepted theory and conventional methodologies, I will also seek answers in the esoterica Stane consulted.

It will not be easy. Unlike him, I cannot read French, and he did not write a single word about the six-fingered hand. All his energies went into deflecting the attentions of the Hounds.

It occurs to me again that Professor Rice could translate the *Livre d'Eibon*, although I have to say, having finally regained the faculty's respect, I hesitate to jeopardize it by instantly reestablishing a reputation for eccentricity.

Perhaps I can think of a reasonable-sounding excuse that will persuade Professor Armitage to grant me access to the restricted collection of the library. Rumor has it that the collection contains some strange, disturbing volumes, and possibly some of those are in English.

I suppose that if I could muster the requisite funds, I could even track down Stane's Mr. Chubinsky, but I will leave that for a last resort. Financial considerations aside, I would prefer to conduct my further investigations without meeting any more sinister characters or otherwise risking life and limb.

Still, I will conduct them no matter what.

Partly my resolution comes from "true scientific curiosity," as dear Bernadine once put it, but partly, I am worried. Obviously, Eibon was capable of predicting what I saw in the heavens, but even so, why bother to record it? Why, unless it was of some practical importance to people living in this age? If it is, then someone had better find out more about it, and—for better or for worse—it appears I have been elected to do so.

THE INVESTIGATORS OF

ARKHAM HORROR

TALES of ADVENTURE and MADNESS

SEE THE

WORLD

THROUGH

OTHER EYE

With lavish art and haunting tales,
The Investigators of Arkham Horror gra
you greater access than ever before to
minds, lives, and adventures of the
investigators from the acclaimed
Arkham Horror Files games.

Witness the 1920s through their eye
travel to the far-flung corners of the Ea
and encounter the unspeakable horror
the Cthulhu Mythos.